EDITED BY
WILLIAM JOHN ROSTRON

CONTENTS

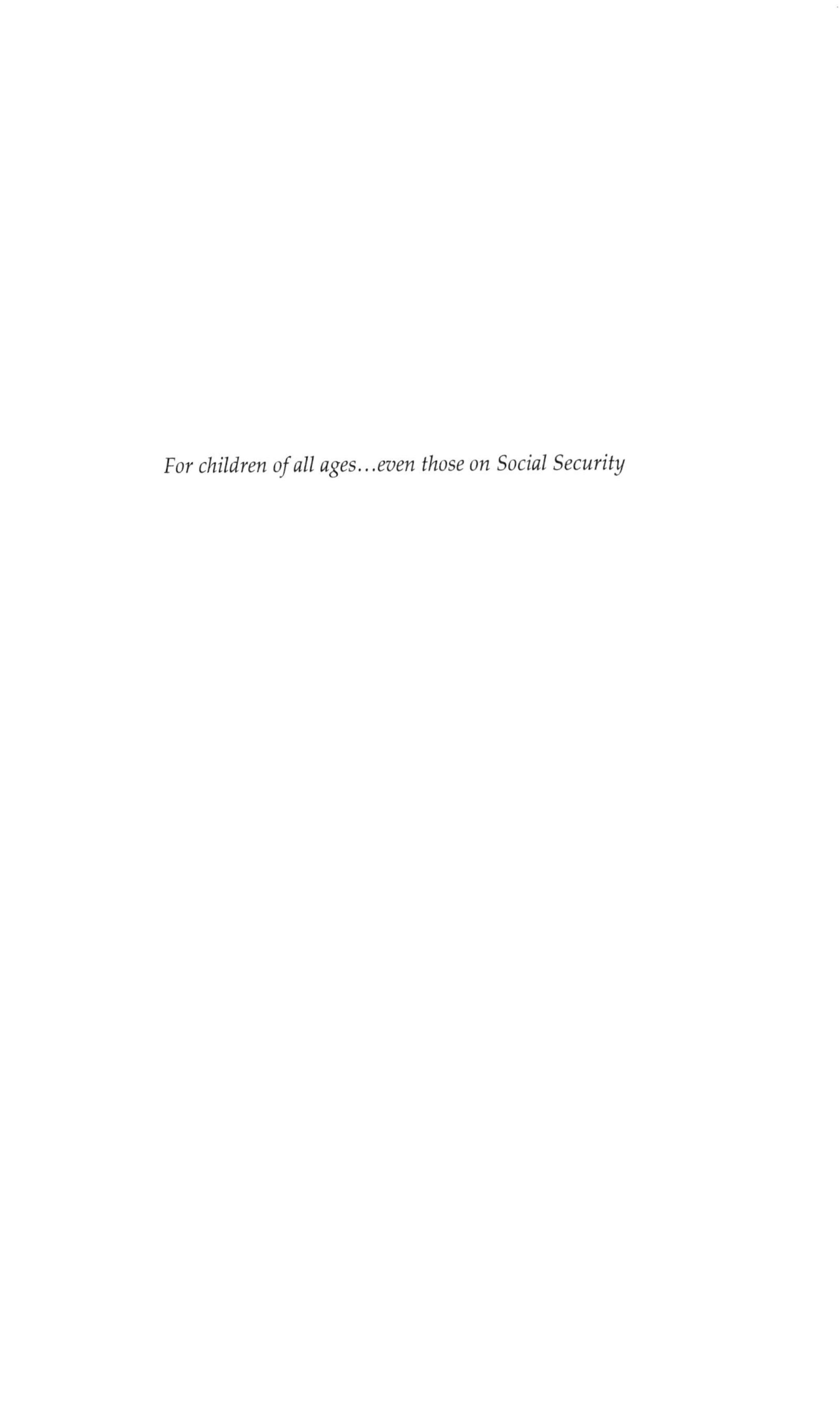

For children of all ages…even those on Social Security

"Superman or Green Lantern ain't got a-nothin' on me.

I can make like a turtle and dive for your pearls in the sea."

Sunshine Superman

-Donovan Leitch

PROLOGUE

HEROES THE GREAT

The term superhero can mean many different things to different people. The classic definition would involve some sort of extra human (super) power that is used to help either one individual, or all of humanity (hero), and this book does skew toward that traditional point of view. There are stories of well-known figures who roam the world of comic books, movies, TV, and computer games, and many of our authors have vividly described that point of view.

However, superhero status can also be bestowed on ordinary people who inhabit our daily lives. People with no spectacular super-power who still manage to be brave and selfless in the light of the tasks and responsibilities they are given. KAPOW also seeks to acknowledge those individuals who go above and beyond what is expected and thus can also proudly evoke the title of "superhero."

This book is a tribute all those real and imagined stars of our world. To this editor the effect of superheroes in my life was very real. Decades ago, fictional beings came into my life and unalterably transformed it through various means. That is the reason that I am so proud to present this look at the world of superheroes. How that happened to me is perhaps unique. But each of us has a story and this is mine.

COMIC BOOKS TAUGHT ME TO READ.

Of that absurd statement, I have no doubt. I was eight years old when I picked up my first *Superman* comic and became obsessed with the entire cosmos of superheroes. I needed to know every facet of their origins, powers, and relationships. It lured me into a world that I would never see the likes of again.

But responsible for my reading skills? For 35 years as an elementary school teacher, I taught children how to read. I knew all the methods available for a child to reach the peak of their abilities. Yet, one indisputable fact emerged. The more children read, the better they became at it. Like every other skill in life, practice makes perfect. While coming to this conclusion, I self-analyzed what had led *me* to be a reader of roughly sixty books a year. I realized that it had been the comics that had made me into a voracious reader. I concluded that as a teacher, I would find a way to encourage my students to read more of what they *wanted* to read. I would reward them for outside reading…any outside reading. This sometimes included directions to the latest video game they had purchased or an entire TV Guide. Magazines, Manga books, cereal boxes, and, yes, comics were all in the realm of class credit. The bottom line was that I was recreating what comics had done for me.

COMIC BOOKS TAUGHT ME TO BE CREATIVE.

I can still picture eight-year-old Billy springing off the backboard of his bed onto the mattress below. My blue pajamas and red towel cape offered no protection from the impact. But I was a superhero saving the world from the likes of any number of villains who had somehow found their way to my bedroom. There was no time for worrying about painful injuries. However, I was more than just re-creating what I had read, I was also trying to visualize new storylines. How could I expand on what professionals had presented, or better yet, how could I create new themes…even new superheroes?

At nine, I created Dartman. Armed with about ten darts, I roamed my bedroom, bringing the unholy to their knees. On a distant wall lay a dartboard that I would target at the designated "bad guy." However, Dartman didn't throw darts standing erect and aiming like in a barroom contest. No, he threw them while flying through the air, lunging at a villain, or avoiding the evil creature's weapons. He threw them sidearm, underhand, and through his legs. Dartman eventually was defeated when the super-villains named Mom and Dad noticed innumerable holes in the walls. (Dartman wasn't very accurate!!!)

COMIC BOOKS TAUGHT ME TO WRITE AND EDIT.

When I was eleven, Robert moved in three doors away from me. Though I had many friends in my Queens neighborhood, none shared my love of comics before he came along. We spent hours reliving our favorite stories or news of upcoming events. What new superhero would DC Comics create, or what was this new company called Marvel, and how would they ever compete with DC?

Eventually, we came upon a comic fan magazine which combined information with a touch of original stories. At eleven, we decided we could do that. We spent hours culling rumors and information about upcoming comics for our gossip column. However, more than that, we created our own original superheroes. I created Miracal Man (which Robert reminded me was misspelled). He was my editor, and I was his as we produced that fan magazine titled "Heroes the Great." We thought we were really innovative by changing the order from "Great Heroes" to "Heroes the Great." We worked untold hours on our project. We then put a notice in the then-most famous comic fan magazine—"Alter Ego." We were ecstatic when we sold our first (and only copy) to a stranger who ordered by mail. We had to produce it by typing the whole magazine with carbon paper attached. Robert could actually type, so he took on the brunt of that task.

John Lennon once said, "Life is what happens while you are busy making plans." By fourteen, I began to be overwhelmed with the many joys and burdens that consume teenagers and adults. I had a challenging academic schedule, played on the school's baseball team, and performed in a rock band around New York City. And then there were girls!

Often, I sat in my bedroom gazing at my comic collection and longed for the simpler times that the comic books represented. But as the Beatles sang, "O-Bla-di, O-Bla-da, Life goes on."

I never lost that love of reading, creating, or writing. I have published dozens of non-fiction articles and three dozen published short stories, most of which are in my short story compendium entitled *A Flamingo Under the Carousel*. In addition, that imagination that I owe entirely to my comic book journey created four novels (*Band in the Wind, Sound of Redemption, Brotherhood of Forever, and The Other Side of the Wind*). Though there are no superheroes in my books, there are innumerable references to people I believe acted with superhuman courage, loyalty, and empathy.

And Robert? We have kept in contact, and he is in this book, so I get to edit him for the first time since "Heroes the Great" (six decades ago). What goes around, comes around.

KAPOW is meant to illuminate *each* of its contributor's personal vision of superheroes in every form of media. Enjoy.

William John Rostron, Editor
   www.WilliamJohnRostron.com

PART ONE
POETRY

POETRY IN MOTION

"I love every movement
There's nothing I would change
She doesn't need improvement
She's much too nice to rearrange."

-Johnny Tillotson

CAPED CRUSADERS

DAVION MOORE

From trauma and misery,
Often society's periphery,
They raise to change the history,
Wearing a mask of mystery,
Their intentions silvery,
Golden hearts of empathy,
Unearthly strength of muscles chivalry,
Here comes justice special delivery,
Putting villains in pillory,
Heroines and Heroes running, flying, striving for victory.

I NEVER DREAMED OF BATMAN

WILLIAM JOHN ROSTRON

When I was young, I'd be…
Superman
Leaping buildings in a single bound

Sometimes, I mimicked…
Flash
The fastest man around

But I never dreamed of Batman

In my room, I imagined…
Spiderman
Climbing a wall

I envisioned…
Green Lantern
The brightest light of all

But I never dreamed of Batman

In fantasy…
The Human Torch
Consumed with fire

Or maybe…
Hawkman
If flying was my desire

But I never dreamed of Batman

Club in hand, I was…
Thor
With his Hammer of Power

Sometimes, I could be
Aquaman
But only in the shower

But I never dreamed of Batman

Able to change size…
Antman
Shrunk so small

Powerful and smart…
Iron Man
Avengers, he led them all

But I never dreamed of Batman

Whether DC or Marvel
I was always a fan

The superhero didn't matter…
But never Batman

Because I never dreamed of Batman

No…Batman was too human
No superpower theme
If I couldn't be really special
What good is it to dream

IF I COULD

CARMEN WHITE

When I was a kid, I hated superheroes.
I wondered, why do they dress so brightly?
Why do they talk in catchy phrases?
Why must they always punch the bad guys?
And why, for goodness sake, does no one ever stay dead?
But I'm all grown up now.
I watch the news as adults are supposed to.
But I find everything so unfair and scary.
I cry and think;

I'd fix it all if I could.

If I could, I'd shine some brightness
on this dark and dreary world.
If I could, I'd say something so perfect
It would change everything for everybody.
If I could, I'd zap bad guys in the face
to make sure all children come home safely.
If I could, I'd bring back my real-life heroes,
And ask them how I can be as strong as they were.

But I can't.

I can't change an entire world.
So, I teach my children to be kind.
I smile for them when I don't want to.
I say a comforting word
and tuck them safely into bed.
Then I go read about superheroes
because
they are the only people left
Who can protect a scared adult?

WHY I STAYED IN ELEMENTARY SCHOOL

LINDA TROTT DICKMAN

It has been an endless
parade of sparkles, princesses, fairies,
knights, ghostbusters,
superheroes, members of the rebel alliance,
worst nightmares, best dreams,
homemade wonder -
and the stories, oh the stories
of wise words and houses of wisdom
of Cinderella and dragons,
of running start hugs
and back office tears,
of being called out, and being
included always as one of them,
always as one of them,
always,
as
one
of
them.

MY SUPERHEROES

HENRY VINICIO VALERIO MADRIZ

Her noble heart is full of love,
to share and unite our family.

Her hands were made to give,
touching our souls intimately.

His alert mind is full of advice,
to guide and serve our future.

His body was made so divine,
to keep dreams with no suture.

In an earthy life lent by God like a blink of wonders
discovering, laughing, learning, sobbing, wandering
we happily and fearlessly go because our founders
and superheroes, called parents, open daily living.

Let's pledge here and now as their trusting children
obedience, respect, loyalty, care, and understanding,
as their heroic offspring of a renewed Justice League.

PART TWO
FICTION

DEAR MR. FANTASY

"You are the one who can make us all laugh
But doing that you break out in tears
Please don't be sad if it was a straight mind you had
We wouldn't have known you all these years"

-Traffic

DOC METEOR, SAVIOR OF THE SPACEWAYS

ERIC ESQUIVEL

Few people talk about how hard it jostles your arm bones when you fire a positronic ray- gun at its maximum setting. But, then again, only a few people had reason to fire one in the first place. Because most people (all but one, actually) weren't the notorious "Doc Meteor, Savior of the Spaceways" ...or whatever the public relations gals back at Meteor Inc. were calling him these days.

Doc knew that the pulps, the comic books, and the sugary breakfast cereals were what funded his entire space exploration operation. But there were days when his youthful depiction in those lurid flights of fancy contrasted with the reality of his situation hard enough to make him cringe. Doc Meteor had been in the Scientist Adventurer game for decades. And, though the illustrators who embellished his adventures wanted the public to believe that the only sign of age he had picked up in all time were a couple of handsome, salt-and-pepper streaks in his hair, the truth was that he had very much begun to feel his age. Not just in the pre-arthritic bones of his ray-gun arm...but also in his soul.

Doc Meteor's occupation, more often than not, made him the point man for mankind's first contact with impossible, one-of-kind, inter-stellar beings. And that was a phenomenal honor... about sixty percent of the time. The other forty percent of the time, the good doctor was called upon to—for the safety of the people of Earth— unholster the aforementioned positronic energy pistol and blast a smoking hole into the very being he was trying to introduce himself to.

It took a lot out of a man executing miracles. And so, before he was forced to kill another one, ol' Doc Meteor screamed through

the microphone of his universal translator at the giant, glowing, extraterrestrial crustacean who was attempting to cut him in half with one of its many pincers: "I come in peace. Don't force me to hurt you. My people only mean to ask what your business is in our solar system!"

Suddenly, the crab-like creature paused. It closed its massive claw and used it to gesture first towards Doc Meteor's translation device, then back towards itself. Doc arched an eyebrow as he removed the uni-translator from his neck and handed it to the monster who had tried to violently murder him only moments ago.

The crab clacked its slimy mandibles together. And the translator deciphered that as: "My word! I'm terribly sorry for the miscommunication, sir. To my eternal embarrassment, I thought that you were...well...food. I had no idea that you—such a tiny, soft thing—were in possession of higher reasoning capabilities." Doc Meteor smiled in anticipation of the long night of diplomatic conversation that lay ahead of him. Sometimes, this job made him feel young again.

MY MARVELOUS LEG!

ALEX GREHY

The anesthetist smiles – she's not wearing her mask, which is sad. All superheroes should wear masks.

"Can you count backward from a hundred?" she asks.

"Seriously, lady, I'm eight, I've been counting forever." I roll my eyes, "OK, one hundred, ninety-nine, ninety-eight, ninety-sev…"

Last week I was kicking a football around the block with Fred, he's my best friend. When we got tired, we sat on a bench in the park, talking about the universe – our soccer super-universe. We were talking, again, about which superheroes we'd have on our soccer team. We reckon the ones that look weak but are strong inside would be the best 'cause they're fast an' cunning. The big toughies could just run right over the other players – stomp 'em and squash 'em! But if they kicked for a goal, the ball'd go right through the net and right on through every building in the block. I mean, we get in enough trouble for kicking a ball 'round the streets, but knocking holes in people's walls? Ooof!

"Superfast or superstrong?" asked Fred, "you gotta be one or the other. That's the rule, and we agreed on that first."

"FAST!" I shouted and took off down the street, laughing.

"Wait for me!" shouted Fred behind me.

It was then my leg broke. BAM! It just snapped! I tried to meditate like those mystic monk heroes, but it hurt so bad. The doctor tells Mom it was serendipity. We wouldn't have found IT otherwise. Mom said that meant I'd got a lucky break. Yeah, hilarious, Mom.

I got to stay in the hospital with my own room and a TV. Fred's mom brought him to visit. Our moms went off to cry in the cafeteria, which was fine by us.

"It's my fault your leg broke. I'm sorry," Fred says, looking at his feet.

"But you weren't anywhere near me!"

"I wished for you to trip up so I could catch up with you."

"Nah! You're the noble type – even if you think bad things, they turn to good." I look around the hospital room and pull his head near to mine. "See, my leg's got an ancient evil growing in it, and your wish made it show itself. Now that's a superpower." I whisper.

Fred looks properly impressed.

"Tomorrow, the doc's gonna whack it and zap it, and I'm going to go bald just like the best wise men."

"Hey, if you're bald, then your hair can't block your psychic powers – maybe you can kick the ball with your mind."

We high-five. That sounds pretty cool. He hands me a pack of candy, and we chew for a while.

"Can I tell you a secret?" I ask.

"Course! You can trust me."

"I'm scared. I don't know what's happening. Mom keeps crying, and the doctor says he'll try to fix me. They say I'm brave, but I don't know what I'm being brave about."

I'm trying not to cry.

"S'okay." said Fred, "All superheroes have that one thing that scares them; it makes them more powerful."

"Huh?"

"Yeah! Brave people get scared of stuff, but they do it anyway."

Our moms come in, and their faces are red and blotchy.

"Good luck, honey," says Fred's mom.

Fred waves, "See ya next week."

Mom sits on the bed. "Listen, sweetie, I've got to sign some papers so the doctor can fix your leg. Are you OK with that?"

I wonder whether to tell her that I'm scared or don't understand, but then I think about my favorite superheroes.

"Yeah, mom. Let's whack it and zap it!"

She smiles. "You're so brave. It's for the best, I promise."

I wake up – everything looks all floaty and funny, like when superheroes are chasing bad guys between dimensions. I try to sit up, but something's not right. I look down.

They cut my leg off! They whacked it good!

I wonder whether the doctor can make me a whizzy wheelchair with lasers and jets and stuff…

GRANDPA'S FANTASTIC FOUR

WILLIAM JOHN ROSTRON

It should have been like any other Sunday at Uncle Jake's. As usual, the whole family gathered there. Three generations of the Ross family loved the time together—the food, fun, and family. However, it was always the pool that was the main draw. The youngest generation, the four cousins, or the "Fantastic Four," as their grandfather always called them, never seemed to step foot on dry land. They couldn't know that they would truly live up to their name on this particular Sunday.

Besides their superhero group name, everyone had been given an individual "Grandpa" nickname. "Will the Thrill" was the oldest at almost 12 and the only boy. He often was the quiet one in the group. His sister and two girl cousins talked so much—mostly about girl stuff. Though slender, he had already attained an adult black belt in Tai-Kwon-do. You would never know it to meet him because he never showed off his abilities.

Next came Samantha or "Sam the Sham." Only two months younger than her first cousin, Will, she had achieved her "Grandpa" name because she could spin tails of fantasy from a young age. No one wanted to call them lies because she never meant to trick anyone but instead make people laugh. Grandpa often called her his little Shammy.

Next came the two "young'uns," Bella-Capri and Ava-Marie. Will's younger sister, "Stellar" Bella-Capri, loved to sing, dance, and put on shows for everyone. She was going to turn six that summer when *it* happened.

A year younger than her cousin, Bella-Capri, Ava "Potatah" Marie got her name because she liked to dress up in disguises, just like the Mr. Potato Head toy she had started playing with at a very young age. Though she still pulled out Potato Head, she had also graduated to a closet full of costumes from Malicifent to the Little Mermaid's Ursula. Ava "Potatah" Marie had a thing for disguises and villains.

Yes, the "Dirty Dozen" (another Grandpa nickname) got together every Sunday. Grandpa and Grandma, *their* three kids and their spouses, and, of course, the Fantastic Four met. They couldn't know that everything would change on this particular day, and Will, Sam, Bella-Capri, and Ava-Marie would be heading for an adventure they would never forget.

A favorite activity was jumping from the four-foot-high stone platform spanning the width of the pool's deep end. Each would take turns seeing who could make the most original motions before hitting the water. It was Sam who thought of a new game that would get them into a mess.

"What if we all jump together at the same time?" asked Sam.

"Sounds good," said Will, but the two younger girls seemed skeptical.

"What if…," started Bella-Capri but was shot down by the stare of the two twelve-year-olds.

"But…" started Ava-Marie—also shot down.

"I heard my father telling Grandpa that he just put a new super filter at the bottom of the pool. It is super powerful and can suck up all the dirt and garbage from the whole pool in five minutes. No one is supposed to be in the pool when it is turned on," offered Will.

"Will, you're exaggerating as usual," cut in Sam.

"No, I'm not. We have to make sure none of our pool toys are in when it is on. Come to think of it, I haven't seen my Nerf football in a while."

"Let's go see," yelled Ava-Marie excitedly.

"No, I don't think that's a good idea," cautioned Bella-Capri, Will's sister, who had also been warned by her father not to go in the pool when the super filter was on.

"What's a matter—chicken?" challenged Ava-Marie, who only minutes before wouldn't even agree to a "group jump."

"Yeah, chicken. Come on, doesn't Grandpa call us the Fantastic Four?" added Sam.

"But we don't have superpowers like the real Fantastic Four," snapped Will. "Besides, it's not *your* dad who will be angry."

"Ava-Marie, check to see if either of them has any eggs underneath them," Sam whispered in her young cousin's ear—loud enough for Will and Bella-Capri to hear. The youngest cousin didn't get the joke for a second and started looking under the brother and sister, making them laugh harder.

"Okay," agreed Will and started to sneak off.

"Where are you going?" Sam looked puzzled.

"If we are going to do this, let's do it right—let's see this giant suction filter in action. I'll turn it on, and we'll all jump together."

"Will, what about your dad," challenged Sam.

"He's busy arguing politics with your dad and Ava-Marie's mom. If we're lucky, we'll jump, see the sights, and return before they even know I turned it on. Ready?" Will ran behind the jump platform, turned on the filter, and then ran and joined his cousins for the big event—an adventure they would never forget.

They held hands with the two little ones in the middle and jumped simultaneously. Their descent into the water was uneventful until they reached the super filter. They soon understood why no one was supposed to be in the pool when it was on. The big square grating at the bottom of the deep end had retracted, and the super-strong suction pulled everything in the pool—including the four cousins!

They quickly descended under the pool's liner and along a system of pipes. They headed toward the giant filter intake, which could have hurt them. Unable to speak while underwater, Will guided them toward what looked like another choice. Sam grabbed Ava-Marie's wrist, and Will held his sister as they held their breath and swam toward a tunnel. In the passageway, they were swept along at a fast pace. Though it seemed like hours, the rushing water washed them onto the shore of an underground river in a matter of minutes. They found themselves in a cave that was only half-filled with water. They could finally breathe. Will and Sam made sure that the younger ones were okay before understanding they still had problems.

They knew they were somewhere deep in the Earth with no apparent entrance or exit. It confused them that they could still see each other, and they soon realized that the rocks on the cave's roof were mysteriously illuminated. They did not have time to consider this phenomenon when Ava-Marie spoke.

"Monsters," she whispered and pointed at the wall. The others looked confused. "Monsters," she repeated, pointing at the rocks against one wall. With that, one of the rocks *blinked* and moved slowly toward them. Filled with fear, they backed up from the wall toward the underground river. The only good news was that the rock people who emerged from the walls moved slowly.

They soon realized that the walls were not stalking them but rather dozens of stone creatures. Some had arms or legs, but some were just misshapen rocks with tiny eyes. The ones who could move did so toward the cousins.

"Here...over here," yelled a high-pitched voice, and Bella-Capri turned toward the water and couldn't believe what she saw. They looked almost human and were about the size of a 6-year-old girl. Their head and body were human-shaped, with the only difference being that they had feathers for hair, and their hands and feet had webs between each of the digits, obviously used for swimming, as a dozen of them were treading water in the underground stream. Only after two of them emerged onto dry land did the cousins notice the small pair of wings each had on their backs.

"Aw, they're cute," giggled Ava-Marie, and Bella-Capri agreed. Indeed, their petite features and large, colorful eyes made them similar to cuddly, doll-like creatures. This fact was especially true when compared to the ugly stone figures slowly approaching them.

"Come with us…quickly," said the leader of the human fish/birds. Will nodded to Sam, and they all jumped into the stream and left the stone monsters behind. They were led into another underground cavern and were stunned by the vision they beheld. Hundreds, perhaps thousands of the human fish/birds were in the water, on the land, and flying up above—and they were all singing!

They smiled for the first time since being sucked underground through the pool filter. It was such a joyous place, with the happy music serving as a background for flying, swimming, and even dancing in the air, water, and land. Ava-Marie and Bella-Capri quickly joined in the dance. Will and Sam held back.

"Something is just too perfect about this place. I just don't know what," whispered Sam to Will.

"I know," answered Will. However, before the conversation could continue, they were approached by a small group.

"Welcome," announced one of the human fish/birds.

"How come you speak English?" asked Will.

"Long story, we'll tell you later," answered the leader.

"Where are we?" questioned Sam.

"Long story," was the answer.

"Who are you?"

"Long…," started the leader but was interrupted by Will and Sam together.

"Yeah, we know a long story."

"Play and have fun with all of us, *Piscavi*. We'll get to the details later." With that, they proceeded to break into some fancy dance moves, which Ava-Marie and Bella-Capri joined in. Even Sam and Will eventually gave in and partied until they were exhausted.

"If we can't beat them, we might as well join them," chuckled Will as he broke into some dance moves of his own. Sam held back for a few minutes but then relented. The day was filled with good times, laughing, singing, and swimming. However, as the nighttime came, everything quieted down. Suddenly, the four cousins were all alone. The two youngest went to sleep while Sam and Will grew restless for answers. They roamed the empty caverns looking for clues and eventually found themselves back where they first came ashore earlier that day.

They could see the stone people, but they seemed to be asleep except for one. He did not frighten them because he made no move toward them but instead moved his hand slowly upward. Finally, when its hand had reached full height, it was pointed at scratched marks on the wall. No, they were words. The message that was written —*Get Out!*

They worked their way back to their younger cousins and tried to figure out what it all meant. If only the stones could talk. Hours later, the cavern again filled up with the Piscavi. Sam didn't wait long to act. She screamed at the top of her lungs.

"It's time for the *long* story."

"Now," added Will, looking as menacing as he could.

"Yeah, now," echoed Ava-Marie and Bella-Capri, though they really didn't care and were merely mimicking their older cousins.

The crowd grew quiet, and the three Piscavi, who seemed like leaders, stepped forward and took turns speaking.

A long time ago…well, we don't know when it was because there is no time down here, we were like you—just ordinary people. We woke one day and found it raining—a rain that never stopped. Soon, our valleys were filling up, and we ran to higher ground, but we soon lost that. The water was coming up as high as the hills. It was evident that soon, there would be no land at all. There was a great wizard at this time, and we all ran to him and asked for help —and he did.

We were all transformed by a spell. Of course, we were initially reluctant, even scared, but we had no choice. We became what you see. The Wizard explained that we could fly above the water, and when we got tired, we could swim in it. It worked, and we survived even though our whole world was flooded. After many, many years, there started to be land.

Most of the time, we just thought of ourselves as people. However, as we traveled the world, we realized that some people had stayed the same. The first ones we ran into were the Romans, who hunted us like animals. To them, we were something they had never seen before, so they called us Piscavi from their Latin language—Pisces for fish and Avis for a bird. It fit, but naming us didn't stop them from hunting us, so we went underground and have been here ever since.

Now, we stay down here most of the time so that we won't be hunted. However, we go into your world now and then to see what is happening and steal food. However, we limit our time up there. And now you know our story.

"When can we go home?" whispered Ava. "I miss my mommy and daddy."

"I don't know if that is possible," the leader and storyteller answered. "No one has ever come down here before."

"Good," announced Sam, "I love it here." However, then she turned to her three cousins behind her and winked.

"Yeah, me too," chimed in Will, turning to the younger cousins and also winking. They didn't get it.

"I want to go home," cried Bella-Capri and Ava-Marie almost simultaneously.

"We will…eventually," mumbled Sam softly and smiled. "We will, but I think they will try to stop us. So, let's play a game and make believe we love it here, so they don't suspect we want to leave."

"Now, I know why Grandpa calls you 'Sam the Sham,' and we learned in school that a sham is like a faker. You are good at this," laughed Will.

"Hey, Grandpa didn't give me the name for nothing," answered Sam, "and aren't we the Fantastic Four?"

Later, Sam hatched a detailed plan and told it to Will. Her life as the Sham had led her to be very creative in her thinking. It was almost like a superpower.

"Okay, here's what we know. There is no time down here, so we don't have to rush. Whenever we go back, nothing will have changed. We probably will be back just after we jumped in the pool."

"But from what they told us, there doesn't seem to be a way back," argued Will.

"No, they told us that 'now and then they go up to the surface.' So, there has to be a way out. We just have to find it."

"I can help," whispered a soft voice from the shadows, and all four cousins turned to look. A small Piscavi stood hiding in the corner. "I'll show you the way—a secret way to the surface that only I know."

When he walked out of the shadows, they noticed that he looked slightly different from most others of his kind. His feathers and skin were grayish, and he moved slowly compared to most Piscavi.

"Why?" asked Will.

"Yeah, all the others don't seem to want us to go," chimed in Sam.

"You look funny," chuckled Bella-Capri, and she and Ava-Marie started laughing.

"It's not nice to laugh at people," Will yelled at the two young ones.

"It's okay. I won't look like this for long. Let me start at the beginning. I am Saxum, the only one left who knows the importance of my name."

"Now I'm confused," remarked Sam.

"The young ones of my kind didn't mean to mislead you. They just don't know the truth. I am the last of *my* kind.

"C'mon, there are still many Piscavi out there—hundreds, maybe thousands. Aren't there?" questioned Will.

"No, I am the last of the original Piscavi. There were millions of us when the flood came. I am the last of those adults who made a deal with the Wizard. You see, he didn't just help us because he was nice. There was a price for him saving us."

"What price?" asked both Sam and Will.

"After a Piscavi has had 12 years or 4,280 days in the sun…he or she turns into stone."

"The stone people!"

"Yes, those are all the Piscavi of the past," mumbled Saxum. The Wizard was clever. He knew that the Earth would eventually need land, so one by one, we became that land. We all understood the deal and accepted it. What choice did we have?

"So, what is happening to you?" asked Sam.

"Well, I have had 4,279 in the sun. My next trip up is my last. That's why I haven't been up there since those people came in their wooden ships. I think you call them Pilgrims. In fact, I think the rock that they landed on was my uncle." He smiled. "Well, maybe."

The young ones started to laugh, but Sam and Will gave them a stern look.

"Your story is so sad," sighed Sam.

"No, it's not. I have had a very long life. We all have down here, and you may not have had any land to come down to us from if we had not created it. Even the young ones have been around for a long time. But not as long as me. I am the last of the old-timers. These young ones don't remember the deal with the Wizard because it was so long ago, and they were all too young. Still, they have had many, many years of enjoying life. When their time comes, it comes. But that time shouldn't come for you four."

"What do you mean?"

"My name was not always Saxum. When all the Piscavi older than me died, I asked the younger ones to call me by that name. None of them could remember the Roman language, so I took their word for "stone" to be my name to remind me that, eventually, I would be joining all the friends I knew. However, the Wizard's spell could affect you four. He believed there was something special about the number 12, so he made the spell for 4280 days. He knew that was exactly twelve years. Of course, when we went underground, those days stopped being counted because there is no time down here. They only get counted when we go up. It takes hundreds of years, maybe even thousands, to reach the number."

"So don't go up," said Will.

"No, now and then we need food, things, or just to play. But, if I'm right, this spell affects you too, and probably the opposite way."

"Huh?"

"If you are down here on the 4280th day of your life, you become part of us…you fall into the same spell. Because *all your days* have been spent above, you would change on that day—your 12th birthday."

Will tried to hide the fact that he was scratching a rough spot that developed on his arm. However, Sam noticed.

"Will, we were having the party today, but isn't your *real* birthday tomorrow?"

Bella-Capri and Ava-Marie had not been paying attention to the conversation but had heard the last statement that Sam had made. They started to sing "Happy Birthday."

"Not now," yelled Sam, more in frustration than anger. Will scratched the gray spot on his arm.

"Time to get out, and I think I have a plan," announced Sam.

"I hope so," whimpered Will.

The four cousins, along with Saxum, gathered and discussed their scheme. When they were done talking, they all knew what to do.

"Attention, all Piscavi, in gratitude for your friendship and hospitality, Bella-Capri would like to entertain you with a song and dance recital," announced Saxum. Though she was a good performer, it was all meant as a distraction. Bella-Capri put on a ballet, tap, and hip-hop dancing show and sang a song from the "Little Mermaid." Most of the Piscavi population sat captivated. Sam's plan called for the rest of them to find their way toward the exit shown to them by Saxum. Sam, Will, and Ava-Marie snuck away and covered most of the route. However, they knew the Piscavi would catch on eventually, so they had to use other tricks.

"Where are your cousins?" yelled a voice from the audience.

"Yeah, how come they don't want to see you dance?

"Something funny is going on here?"

Singing and dancing were Bella-Capri's superpowers. Lying was not.

Saxum knew that the deception was over. He quickly flew to the stage, had Bella-Capri grab his legs, and flew off toward the escape route. As the other Piscavi tried to follow, they had trouble getting in the air. As part of the "celebration," Sam and Ava-Marie had baked fruit cakes for the crowd to eat—very, very, heavy fruit cakes. With mostly human bodies, the Piscavi were not great flyers, and the extra weight kept them pinned to the ground. Still, they started to run toward the exits. There were two directions the crowd had to choose from, and they were helped with the decision by a rather unusual-looking member of their *flock*.

"They went that way. I saw them. They went that way. Hurry, go left."

Unable to fly, they all ran through the left exit. Ava-Marie quickly removed the Piscavi costume she had created from leftover feathers and cloth. She smiled at her superpower of deception. She then ran down the right exit to catch up with her cousins. Within a few feet, she passed by Will, who was the rear guard. Two Piscavi stragglers soon came into the tunnel. They had not been at Bella-Capri's dance recital and so hadn't been sent in the wrong direction—or had heavy cake. While his cousins made their way up the surface to freedom, Will stood against the two flying searchers.

"What are you going to do from down there," taunted one of the Piscavi while hovering about three feet above Will, while the other flew a bit lower to get a laugh by tweaking Will's nose. Instantaneously, Will's right hand shot up with the speed he had exhibited while attaining his black belt in Tai-Kwon-do. Before the first Piscavi had even hit the floor from his punch, Will lifted his foot three feet above his head and planted a kick in the other Piscavi's stomach. As they groaned on the floor, Will ran to catch up with his cousins. Sam and Ava-Marie were almost at the surface when Saxum flew Bella-Capri to the exit. Will ran for the exit, but he was too late. Five Piscavi had come in from a side entrance and blocked his path to the cave exit. With his "super" skills, he might take on two or three of them, but five would be able to keep him from getting out, especially since they would soon be joined by the rest of the crowd that had now found their way.

Sam and Ava Marie stood in the fresh air and were helping Bella-Capri through the opening when they saw Will's dilemma. And Saxum saw it, too. He left Bella-Capri and flew to Will. He lifted him up and flew higher and higher, followed closely by the five pursuers. If he could only stop and let Will off, the boy could climb out—but there was no time. Saxum's only choice was to fly straight out of the cave.

"No," screamed Will, "you'll…

In the real-time of the Earth, the four cousins had only been gone a few minutes. Their parents hadn't even noticed when they walked into the backyard from the street. The cave exit had only been in the woods down the block from Will and Bella-Capri's home.

"Oh, there you guys are. It's time for lunch. The doctor doesn't want Grandpa to eat red meat, so we're trying something different. So, you have your choice of tilapia or Cornish hens," announced Uncle Jake.

"What are those?" groaned Bella-Capri.

"Think of it as fish or birds," answered Uncle Jake.

"No, thank you, screamed the four cousins all at once.

As the sun set, the family went to the front of the house. There, Uncle Jake made a ceremony of taking down the American flag from the pole. After serving in Afghanistan, he returned home and put up the flagpole.

They laughed when Grandpa yelled at them to join in.

"C'mon, my Fantastic Four. This is important."

"We actually are a Fantastic Four. We really were superheroes because today...," Ava Marie blurted out before Sam put her hand over the youngest cousin's mouth. Their Grandpa didn't notice this action but reacted to Ava's words.

"You sure are to me. But...," their grandfather said as he looked up at the flag, "So are the ordinary people who defended that through the years." He pointed to the descending flag. The four cousins stood quietly with Bella-Capri giving a small salute, which the others soon copied. As they started to leave, only the Fantastic Four noticed something strange.

Through the years, Uncle Jake had added to the landscaping of the area little by little—bushes, decorative mulch, flowers, and, this year, some large boulders from a nursery. As the dozen members of the Ross family looked on, the flag made its descent. After he folded it, they all mulled around, ready to say their goodbyes, when Jake spoke.

"I could have sworn that I only ordered four large stones…but there are five!"

Sam, Will, Bella-Capri, and Ava-Marie, Grandpa's Fantastic Four, smiled and looked on as one of the stones *winked* at them.

HOW TO BE A FAMOUS SUPER VILLAIN

STEVEN MICHAELS

The following skit imagines what Three Notorious Retired Supervillains would do if it turned out that their grandkids didn't have the gruesome gumption they had. (Note: the names of these villains have been changed to protect the innocent from copyright infringement).

Enter Joke Man Jr., son of the infamous Joke Man, supervillain and comedian of crime.

Joke Man Jr.: I'm sorry, Dad, but I've tried everything, and Joke Man Jr. Jr. is just not bad enough.

Joke Man: How can you say that? I vowed that anyone descended from me, the Joke Man, would be the most notorious villain of all time. What's wrong with him?

Joke Man Jr.: He's too nice. He only wants to use exploding whoopie cushions that make small bangs. He's afraid it will make the other kids cry!

Joke Man: Disgraceful! How's he supposed to learn to steal candy from babies if he's afraid of making people cry?

Joke Man Jr: I dunno Pop, but you got to do something. And it's not just him. It's the other kids, too! They've all gone soft.

Joke Man: Okay, Joke Man Jr. Let me handle Joke Man Jr. Jr. and his little friends; bring them here and leave it all to me. (Joke Man Jr. leaves) Wex Wupor and Queen Queen aren't gonna be too happy when they hear about this.

Enter Wex Wupor, an evil mad scientist, and Harley Queen, the Joke Man's ex-lover; both are thoroughly upset.

Wex Wupor: What is this I hear about our grandkids getting soft?

Joke Man: Oh, hi there, Wex. So, you heard?

Harley Queen: *(holding her club)* Yeah, we heard. How can this be? You and me, Joke Man, were the mirthful monarchs of crime; that's why I changed my name to sound almost like those old-timey pranksters! I can't have my bratty grandkids not living up to such high crime standards. What are we gonna do? *(she sobs)*

Joke Man: There there, Queenie. We'll figure something out.

Wex: (*grumpily*) You better. I enjoy being a retired supervillain. Do you have any idea how exhausting it was trying to hide from a super-human with X-ray vision?

Joke Man: Oh, I know how it is. And people have the nerve to call me batty! They clearly haven't met my nemesis. He'd come creeping out of the shadows on my one day off a week, throw me against a wall, and say (*darkly*), "I'm on to you, Joke Man." I tell you, that guy had no sense of humor.

Queen: Oh Mr. Puddinghead. Those were good times. But I still can't believe what's happening to our grandkids.

Joke Man: Well, Joke Man Jr. is bringing them here so we can have a little chat and maybe teach them a thing or two. And here they are now.

Enter Joke Man Jr. and the three grandkids.

Joke Man Jr. Jr: (*pretending to be an airplane*) WEEEEEE! Daddy, we are being planes, saving people wherever we go!

Wex Lupor: Good grief! It's worse than I thought! They have cute and colorful imaginations! (*He turns and steps back, too ashamed to face them.*)

Joke Man Jr: I really appreciate this, Pop. *(talking to Jr. Jr.)* Daddy's gonna go rob a bank now! Be super bad for your granddad, Uncle Wex, and Auntie Queenie!

Joke Man Jr. Jr. Oh, yay! I wuv Auntie Hawley Queen!

Joke Man Jr: No, son. Love's too strong a word. You like Auntie as a friend. Remember, a true villain only loves himself. Bye now. *(he exits)*

Wex Jr. Jr. Hey, Joke Man! Do you want to help old people cross the street?

Joke Man: No! We don't help people, silly. We trip them! Now sit here, children, and let me show you. Wex, come here a minute, will you?

Wex Wuthor: All right, but please tell me they've stopped being so darn cute. *(he crosses over to Joke Man, who trips him, and he falls hurt while Joke Man laughs; all three kids begin to cry.)*

Wex Jr. Jr.: *(to Wex)* Grandpa! Grandpa! Are you hurt?

Wex: No, no, I'm fine. *(holding back tears)* Besides, why wouldn't a deranged clown man try to trip me? I should really be more careful.

Joke Man: See kids! Being mean is fun! Why don't you try kicking Auntie Queenie in the shins?

Queen: No way, Joke Man! I just had my knees replaced. Why don't they beat you up instead?

Joke Man: Tempting, but I need to show them how to successfully run away from a crime scene later. And how can I do that if I'm hurt? Wex, you don't mind a bit more thrashing, do you?

Wex: Well. actually–

Joke Man: *(ignoring him entirely and talking to the kids)* A quick motion is all you need. *(He stomps on Wex's foot).*

Wex: Ow! I thought you were gonna kick me in the shin?

Joke Man: Important Super Villain Lesson: never do what is expected of you!

Wex: Oh, do you mean like this *(pretends to throw a punch to the face, Joke Man dodges, and Lex throws a left instead to the gut)*

Joke Man: *(groaning in pain)* See, kids. It's easy! *(falls to the floor, and kids begin to cry again)*

Queen: *(to the kids)* Now don't start that again! Why do you gotta be such babies?

Queen Jr. Jr.: Sorry, Grandma, but we are only four!

Queen: So what? That just means double the terrible twos! Where's your fighting spirit?

Joke Man Jr. Jr. Ooo. I know what you mean! Like Mr. Bat, Guy is always fighting crime and stopping evildoers in their tracks.

Joke Man: *(annoyed and appalled)* Did you just say, Mr. Bat Guy? How dare you!

Queen: Easy there puddinghead! That Mr. Bat Guy can be pretty rough. Maybe we should take a page or two from his book to teach the kids.

Wex: Right. Right! Let's channel those dark voices. Okay. Repeat after me, kids: *(intense growling)* "I AM THE NIGHT"

The kids begin crying again. "No, no! Mr. Bat Guy too scary!"

Joke Man: *(also crying)* Yeah, cut it out! You want to give me nightmares or something!?

Wex: This is going nowhere! Perhaps if we tinkered with their DNA a bit. I'll go get my needles! *(he exits)*

All three kids scream: NO! NO! Needles bad! (and run wildly about.)

Joke Man: *(trying to settle them down)* It's okay! Pain is good, remember?

Queen: *(outraged)* That's exactly what you told me when you pushed me in that vat of chemicals! But it certainly wasn't good! (*She bops him on the head with her club*). See what I mean?

Joke Man: Come on, Queenie; can't you take a joke? *(he begins to act woozy.)*

Queen: I've been taking a joke for about 30 years now, and I've about had it. I used to be a doctor, for crying out loud. A doctor! Do you know how much money I made? Instead, you had me robbing banks and fleeing the crime scene with comical money bags with dollar signs, which proved to be nearly empty as you'd already taken your share!

Joke Man: (*chuckling*) Now that's funny!

Queen: *(enraged)* Then how come I'm not laughing! (*she bops him on the head again, enough to make him unconscious.*)

Wex: Good news, I found my needles. Who wants to become a science experiment? *(the kids run off stage screaming.)* Wait, come back. I promise you'll each have an imperfect clone for a friend or enemy–it's all in how you talk to them. Come back! (*Exits*)

Queen: *(taking out her cell phone and making a call)* Hello! Mr. Bat Guy. Mr. Dark Evening. The Joke Man's ready to go back to the retirement home now. Oh, and tell that cute bird friend of yours I said hello. *(she drags him off stage.)*

SUPERPOWERED CHILL GAS STATION VIBES – 24 SONGS, 1 HOUR 43 MINUTES

BEA SAGE

Band-aids should be sold at every gas station. Right? I know they're sold at *some*; this ain't my first gas-station-bandaging rodeo, but stock is shockingly irregular. So instead of just picking up a little box of Disney band-aids aimed at 3-to-5-year-olds (because I deserve a treat), I'm standing in the aisle, bag of chips and gummy worms dangling from one hand, attempting to figure out the practicality of using tissues and tape – both things they do, in fact, stock – to patch up the cut on my arm that won't stop fucking bleeding. It's unfortunate the whole superpowers schtick didn't come with super healing for me. Super healing would've been really useful. Also unfortunate that my handler, Shana, is on the other side of town. She's the only person I'd trust to have actual bandages. Then again, she'd want to debrief, and I prefer to think as little as possible about my fights after they've finished.

I ditch the tape idea, but I take a little plastic-wrapped tissue packet and head for the counter – quick detour to the fridges, grab an energy drink – maybe I'm just delaying because I *know* the clerk's going to look at me weirdly. I mean, you would too if you were faced with a mousy five-foot-nothing twenty-some girl in your gas station in the middle of the day with bruises all over her face. In my defense, I could also use the electrolytes.

Between the chips, lollies, tissues, and drink, I've about reached the limit of what I can carry, so I head to the counter, dump it all down, and add a chocolate bar. What? I need the sugar. I *deserve* the sugar. Fighting shapeshifters fucking sucks. One of the things I'm good at is predicting my opponent's moves, and it's a little difficult to do that when they can grow themselves an extra goddamn arm in the middle of the fight.

The clerk pulls my things over to scan them and asks, "You okay?" She's looking at me, sure enough, weird.

"Roller derby," I lie easily. "Gonna go home and ice it all now." The second part isn't a lie, at least.

She's about my age, which means she luckily takes that as an answer and moves on. Older people usually either fuss or start asking questions.

She scans everything in silence, then reads out my total to me. The moment I hand her almost all the money from my pockets – the super-hero gig isn't exactly cash-rich, even when you've just been defending a government building and rightfully should've been tipped – there's a loud hammering noise on the roof.

I jump, muscles tensing. I've settled into a combat stance and done a rapid check of myself, trying to figure out how much juice I have left – answer, not fucking much – before the noise settles into a rhythm, and I realise it's rain.

The clerk's looking at me even *weirder* now. She may be bumping up against the real explanation for the bruises, but with any luck, she just thinks I'm a jumpy skater. I relax, slightly shaking my shoulders, and gather my things with a sheepish smile. And promptly realise that the rain is going hardcore out there; my bus stop is a ten-minute walk away, and I do not want to do that. I renew the smile and gesture at the aisle behind me with my drink. "You gonna kick me out if I crash here until the rain stops?"

She shakes her head—chatty woman. I lower myself to the ground – carefully – and arrange myself against the aisle, attempting to find a position that doesn't involve any sharp corners or dull bruises. Luckily, there are little stuffed sheep in the baskets next to me, and I grab a couple of them and stuff them behind my back. Then the remaining ones start staring at me really judgmentally, and I feel guilty about it. I pop another one into my jacket pocket, like pseudo-hugging one of them is going to transmit some kinda voodoo power to the others.

The clerk is just watching me. I bother to squint at the nametag on her starchy blue shirt for the first time, which tells me her name is Claire. "Hi, Claire," I say, and she frowns at me for a second before looking down at her own tag.

"Oh," she says. "Hi."

"I'm Sara," I tell her, shrugging out of one jacket sleeve, opening my tissues, and peeling the black cloth of my shirt carefully up away from the cut. I only wince a little, which I'm taking as a win.

Johnny Cash is informing me over the speakers that he's headed for Jackson and has firm plans to mess around when he gets there. Someone likes their music vintage. "This your music choice?" I ask.

"Uh, no. Last clerk. Left their playlist going."

"You into it, or can you just not be bothered to change it?" I carefully dab at the cut with one tissue, which quickly becomes soaked red and falling apart, so I abandon that route and just grab a handful of them, pressing firmly down and hoping it'll close up before I run out of tissues and have to buy another pack. Apparently, it was only my shirt and jacket that had been stopping me from bleeding all over Claire's nice clean gas station.

Speaking of, she finally seems to gather herself together enough to answer. Her blonde ponytail swings a little as she simultaneously lifts her shoulders in a tiny shrug and tilts her head towards the computer. "It's… it's on Spotify. I don't have an account, so- I don't hate this."

"Fair enough." I don't hate it either. "Do you listen to music other ways, or are you one of those freaks who does everything in silence?"

Her lips quirk at that, which is the first real hint of an expression I've gotten out of her. "CDs, mostly."

"Old-school."

"I guess. My parents left me their collection. I've added to it."

"They move somewhere?" I ask, which I'm blaming on the blood loss, because the more likely meaning of 'left' immediately hits me.

Sure enough, she looks down at the counter, fidgeting with something behind the computer, and replies, "They died. In the Event."

"Ah. I'm sorry." I feel some kinda personal responsibility in that, even though I obviously had nothing to do with causing the Event. How could I? I'd been a foetus at the time, same as everyone else who came out with powers. Still, I gained something from it – strength, speed, decreased reaction time, and a nice stable, guaranteed government job – while the aftereffects killed so many adults. And badly, the chemicals seeping into mature cells, slowly stopping regeneration, bringing metabolisms grinding painfully to a halt. I'd been doubly lucky – not only had I gotten powers, but both my mothers had survived.

"Yeah," Claire says and sits down hard on the bench behind her, narrowly avoiding knocking the cigarette packets off the shelf. "Not much else to say, huh?"

"...No."

"Mm. What's your team?"

I blink. "What?"

"Roller derby. What team?"

"Oh. Wildcats," I say, curse myself lightly, and hope to God she's not a High School Musical fan. Or at least believes that a roller derby team would name themselves after a High School Musical team.

"I don't know them."

"Well, we're small," I bluff. "I am no expert yet." I wave my free hand at myself and realise the arm seems to have stopped bleeding. I ease the tissues off, sigh in relief when all that happens is a little stinging, and drop them onto the plastic they were in originally. Doris Day is now bemoaning her past Shanghaian statements and recounting her rice allergy. I'm sensing a theme in these songs, and the theme is 'I'm old, and I fucked up my relationship.'

Still, it provides a convenient excuse for me to redirect the conversation. I jump up, grabbing my energy drink and lollies, and gesture at the computer Claire's still half-hiding behind. "I've got an account. You want me to put something else on?"

"Sure." She gets up and takes the couple steps to the waist-high swinging door at the end of the counter, unlatching it. When she steps back, I push through it, wincing as it hits a stinging spot over my hip, and head for the computer.

I click on the Spotify icon and down half of my drink while waiting for it to come up and load itself. Wi-Fi apparently sucks in here, or possibly I'm just drinking very fast.

The title of the playlist currently playing is the name of the first song, which goes a way towards confirming my suspicions of Mx. Last Clerk's age. "You got any preferences?" I ask Claire over my shoulder as I press pause, log out, log in.

"Not classical. Not metal."

I chuckle. "Okay, avoid the extremes." I'm dialing up my chill-out playlist, figuring that's probably appropriate gas station vibes – or at least appropriate Claire vibes. She seems a little… keyed up as a person – when the sound of someone stamping their feet on the mat outside the door drifts in. I hit play, Springsteen starts crooning at us about the Tucson train, and as the door opens, I paste on a customer service smile, fully planning on doing Claire's job for her just for the hell of it. It's not like I ever got to do anything like this before the government snatched me up.

The guy who walks in looks weirdly familiar – the combination of smoke-grey eyes and a bandanna tied around his neck makes him look like he just stepped out of a Western film, and the way he's storming straight for the counter doesn't really alleviate the effect.

"Can we help you, sir?" I ask, automatically backing up one step and wondering if I'll be able to defend both myself and Claire against this guy without revealing my powers if it comes to it.

He squints at me – those eyes look familiar – then turns to Claire. "Lari!" he exclaims impatiently and points at me. Before I can tell him that I'm Sara, he continues, "That's her."

"What?" Claire says. When I look over at her, she's straightened up and is glaring straight back at this guy with frankly more fire than I would have given her credit for. She also looks like she knows him. What the hell is going on here?

The cowboy guy growls. "You just fought her, Lari, you idiot. I followed her here; she lost me a few streets over. Look at her bruises, for Christ's sake."

She just fought- oh. Oh, fuck.

"Do *not* talk to me like that," Claire/Lari/shapeshifter supervillain threatens cowboy guy as I back up against the wall. She's standing between me and the swinging gate she so kindly unlatched for me. He's right on the other side of the counter, so I have no escape route here, but I can at least make sure my back's covered by a nice slab of brick.

"So, do you work here, or was this just a fun little ruse?" I ask Claire/Lari before cowboy guy can respond. He's too old to have powers, but he still looks like he can fight. And I barely have powers right now. She swings to face me, and I mutter a curse under my breath. Shana's always telling me to talk less in these situations.

"You *are* her?" Claire/Lari says. Fuck fuck fuck. I should really listen to Shana more.

"Her? Who's her?" I attempt. "I'm Sara, like I said. You're not gonna rob me?"

I blink once, and there's a hand around my throat, pushing me up against the wall I placed myself against. I'm kinda regretting that move now. Claire/Lari is still standing at the other end of the behind-counter space, but she's stretched one of her arms out like Mrs. Incredible.

I'm putting background clues together now because there's not a lot else I can do – my energy reserves are damn low. My best and possibly only chance here is if they decide I'm more useful alive and take me somewhere I can escape at a later, more well-rested, and possibly fed date. Mr. Cowboy Grey-Eyes wasn't at the fight I just came from, but I've seen him in other fights – he usually has that bandanna tied around his face, and I've noticed him because I always thought it looked kinda sick in terms of general villain outfit choices. As for-

"Your name's Lari?" I manage to say, meaning her grip isn't really as tight as it feels. She's not actually trying to hurt me, just holding me in place.

"Yes," she says, and turns back to Mr. Cowboy. "Go away. Guard the door."

As for Lari, who knows what she really looks like?

"I can do that from here," Mr. Cowboy says.

I know I hit her hard enough to break ribs at one point today, and maybe that's why she seems to have been moving slowly this whole time, but I have no idea if her shapeshifting abilities extend to joining ribs back together. She was seven feet tall earlier, with shaved hair, looking like a middle-aged biker, not an anxious twenty-something orphaned girl.

Hang on. She told me things. I can talk. I'm good at talking.

"Lari?"

She abandons the attempts to get Mr. Cowboy to leave and turns back to me. "Yes?"

Apparently, Lari's as taciturn as Claire was. "Is this about your parents?"

She sneers at me. "What do you care?"

"Hey." I spread my hands, keeping them carefully back against the wall. As I do, I brush the little stuffed sheep that's still in my pocket, bearing witness to this whole catastrophe. "I think it's important to have a good working relationship with the people you're beating up."

"Your parents survived, huh?"

I consider lying, but it doesn't seem like it would get me very far. "Yes."

"Figures."

"So, why?"

She stares at me for a second, then makes a noise something like a growl in the back of her throat. "You know that government you're working for has records, right? They know exactly which corporations released the chemicals that left me like this, that killed my parents, that landed me in a government-sanctioned dump being raised to be their perfect little soldier. They just did nothing about it. Money changed hands, interests were protected, and that was that."

The sneer shifted into a snarl as she speaks, bitterness laced like poison through her words. The worst part is, she's right, I know that. Publicly, the corporations were fined and sanctioned, but in the grand scheme of things, the actual people behind the Event got off essentially scot-free. And part of that was because the government loved the idea of having people like me working for them. Still, "You've hurt people. You've – maybe *you* haven't killed people, but I've had to stop other powered kids from killing people."

"And you haven't hurt people?" she scoffs, and blinks a couple times. Her face melts very disconcertingly, and when it reforms it's almost the same – leading me to think maybe this *is* her actual face – only she's got a huge black eye blooming, a long cut over one cheekbone, and her jaw looks… not broken, but not exactly where it should be.

I suck in a sharp breath and exclaim, "I was trying to stop *you* from hurting people!" I immediately regret it when the chest expansion makes every tiny injury on my torso cry out. I've never had to… see this before on anyone other than myself.

"You were stopping me from breaking into a building and stealing files. I wasn't hurting anyone."

"Yeah, tell that to the security guard you knocked out." I'm attempting to talk without deep breathing now, which is not entirely successful. "He's in the hospital, and they still don't know how bad the concussion is. Not to mention the broken wrist, on his dominant hand. You know what happens to guards who can't shoot guns anymore? They lose their jobs."

She blinks at me again, only this time nothing changes shape. She just looks thrown.

I keep going, attempting to press my advantage. "Yeah. I'm not saying the whole governmental machine is morally righteous or anything, but me personally, I'm a defender. What were you planning to do with those files if you'd gotten them, anyway? I'm guessing you didn't think you could strong-arm anyone into bringing the corporations to justice, and you know as well as I do that leaking them wouldn't do a damn thing. Which only leaves one option."

Apparently, that was the wrong route because her face hardened again. "They'd deserve it."

I sigh. I can't argue with that. "Could you get grey-eyes over there to get me an aspirin? My head is killing me. Also, my arms. And legs. My body is killing me. I wouldn't say no to some food either."

"…I assumed you had super-healing."

"I *wish*. Can you help me petition someone for that?"

My chill-out playlist is still going, and Taylor Swift is singing about invisible strings when she hesitantly takes her hand off my throat, picks up the gummy worms I'd brought in with me back before this whole mess started, and tosses them in my direction, then shrinks her arm back to normal size. Mr. Cowboy makes an unhappy sound, but there's not a lot he can do about it.

My shoulder twinges as I grab the bag, but I don't care. "I owe you my life," I tell her gratefully as I tear it open, then pause. "Literally, I guess, right now."

"Is the guard really going to lose his job?" she asks quietly, and she sounds like Claire again.

"I don't know," I admit. "Could be they set it, and it all works fine. Too early to tell."

"Lari," Mr. Cowboy says warningly, and I jerk a thumb in his direction, keeping my attention focused on Lari.

"What's his stake in this?" I ask her. I can't stop looking at the bruise spreading from her right eye to her temple. I don't even know which punch landed it.

"I'm not the only one who lost people in the Event."

"Okay. Fair enough. Did you say you grew up in a government facility?" I hadn't quite processed that until it seemed less like I was about to be killed.

She glares at me, drawing herself up, then seems to realise it was a genuine question and relaxes back down. "Yes. All of us who lost our parents were. They wanted us for our powers and thought if they had us almost from birth…"

"Oh." I chew a gummy worm slowly, then swallow it. "That's fucked up."

"Eloquent," Mr. Cowboy snarks.

"Hey. I hurt everywhere, okay, grey-eyes. I don't have the energy to be thinking up scathing critiques of government practice."

"My name is Henry."

I squint at him, and shake my head. "Nah. It's grey-eyes or it's John Wayne."

Lari actually laughs at that, even if she does cut it off immediately.

I turn back to her, ignoring John 'Henry' Wayne's glare, and ask, "Are there more of you? Have I fought government orphan kids before?"

She huffs something that sounds almost like another laugh, only way more bitter. "Yes. Most of the people you goons fight are kids like us, who realised what was going on."

I'm not hugely fond of being called a goon, but I still don't feel like it's necessarily a good idea to antagonise her. "That's… What *were* you going to do with the Event records?"

There's a steely glint in her eyes as she responds, "That wasn't what we were looking for. The people in charge, they want to recreate the Event. And they don't particularly care if people die in the process."

My first reaction, before I can stop it, is, "Oh, come on." Yeah, sure, they've been pouring more money into researching how it happened lately, but it's a hell of a leap from that to 'they're trying to recreate it'.

Lari raises her eyebrows. "I thought you just agreed they're 'fucked up'."

"Yeah, but not–" I wave my hands in the air vaguely, sketching out 'deliberately-repeat-the-greatest-disaster-of-our-generation levels of fucked up'.

"We have someone on the inside." She pauses, and swallows hard before correcting, "We had someone on the inside. The government's running out of soldiers. We're not immortal, and some of us turn against them."

That's… true.

"*Some* of us were against them from the start. You know what Henry got when his wife and brother were killed? A pat on the shoulder and an assurance they'd never let anything like that happen again. That was before they realised they could get something out of it."

"You *had* someone?"

It's John Wayne who chimes in with, "They haven't checked in for weeks. No good reason for that."

"Lots of bad ones," Lari adds quietly. Beneath the damage littering her face – the damage I inflicted – she looks very small, and like she's trying not to hope. I suddenly wonder whether their person inside was someone she grew up with.

The worm I'm swallowing goes snake-like in my throat, dry and scaly. They've got every reason to lie to me, but also – if they didn't want me to know what they were doing, why not just kill me? Or even knock me out and leave me somewhere? Lari honestly seems mostly like she just wants me to believe she's doing the right thing.

I'm not convinced about the laissez-faire attitude she seems to think the government has towards the deaths, but– I know our numbers are dwindling. I know upper ranks aren't happy about that. I know they're in contact with the original scientists and businesspeople. And even if they are trying to reduce the death toll, it was so many people after the original event… what if they fucked up? What if they didn't, but they targeted it to kids they could bring up like Lari, trying to brainwash them?

"That information," she says, and she sounds like she can see the toehold she's gotten in my brain. "It's leverage. We can stop it."

"Do you have an actual plan?"

"Do you seriously think I'm going to tell you that?"

So that was a yes. "Does it involve hurting people?"

She shifts on her feet. "I'm sorry about the guard. But we've never killed anyone. That's just random privileged powered kids who go crazy when they figure out what they can do."

I rub my forehead and drop the gummy worms back onto the bench. "So?"

"We don't want to hurt people. Sometimes it's necessary."

I want to protest that, but I'm staring at her face, bold proof in black and green and blue and red that I live my life by the same words. I don't want it to be necessary. "What if it wasn't?"

"What?"

I take a deep breath, trying to stop myself, breathe, think through it before I propose throwing away my nice stable life, betraying Shana. But I keep bumping up against the same images of government orphanages/training facilities, of the news coverage of hospital wards transformed into palliative care for the dying twenty years ago, of the smug faces of the CEOs responsible. Of the woman in front of me. "What if I got you the files?"

Lari stares at me. John Wayne is staring at me too, I can feel his gaze. He's the first one to reply. "Yes."

She turns to look at him. "What makes you think we can trust her?"

He's steady as he says, "I don't know if we can. But it's that or kill her. You've got us in a no-win situation here. For…" he glances at me, then looks back at her. "For his sake, it'd be nice to at least pretend we've got a win out of it."

She turns back to me slowly, blinks. "They'll hurt you. If they find out," she warns.

"But other people won't be hurt any more." I don't know who Lari's thinking of, but for me it's still the guard.

"You'll help people. We'll be able to stop them, if we have those files. You'll save lives," she agrees.

In the end, that's all I want. To be a defender. I shove my hands into my pockets, and once again encounter the sheep. I pull it out and put it on the bench next to me, under the cigarettes. "I'll do it," I tell Lari and John Wayne, watching the sheep. As Lari lets out a breath it sounds like she's been holding the entire time, its judgemental gaze seems to turn approving.

Dobie Gray's telling us that he wants to get lost in rock & roll as I make the decision I know is going to change my life one way or another. What? Real life soundtracks don't always work out exactly how you might want them to.

PART THREE
NONFICTION

IT'S MY LIFE

"It's my life and I'll do what I want
It's my mind, and I'll think like I want
Show me I'm wrong"

-The Animals

PROTECTION FROM MY KRYPTONITE

ROBERT PRIMAVERA

Who was Superman fooling? Really? Dark-rimmed glasses hid his true identity. Maybe Clark Kent bought that ruse. But really? Could any reasonable person think that would work?

As a teenager, I was hooked on comic books, specifically the superheroes that dominated the industry. I gobbled up anything featuring Superman, Batman, Green Lantern, and a long list of other comics from Marvel to DC.

They gave me comfort and provided protection. But from what? Now, as an adult, comics and the movies featuring those same characters no longer interest me. What changed? What was the lure of those hours lost in the comic world? What did those diversions provide?

I had a secret. I, like those legions of superheroes, protected my true identity. I hid my sexuality from my family, friends, and myself. Being gay was not an option. That world, which I glimpsed from the few representations available, was inhabited by either gruff rough men, dressed for combat or men dressed flamboyantly who swished through the landscape. That wasn't me. Or, I hoped, that wasn't me.

I needed to protect myself from exposure. I needed to protect my family from the humiliation. "Those people" were wretched. Those acts were "unnatural." Instinctively, I hid that from those I loved, from those I called friends, and most of all from myself. And that was the model my superheroes provided. I, as they did, shielded myself with an alter ego.

I don't expect anyone to understand this, but that realization of who I was was also hidden from me. As a teenager, I wanted to belong. As a child, I wanted my parents' approval. As a friend, I needed to fit in. When they entered my consciousness, those thoughts and feelings were my enemies…just like the villains the superheroes faced. Suppress them and survive. Suppress them and fit in. Suppress them, and keep that secret safe. Suppress them from myself to stay sane.

I had found an ally, a co-conspirator. My comic book heroes protected themselves from the enemy who would attack them, or hurt their family and loved ones. By hiding in the shadow of those stories for years, I secreted myself there, safe and sheltered. Sheltered from the hateful glances, the ridicule, the shame that such a revelation would visit upon my family. There I stayed until I realized, like Mr. Kent, those glasses were really not fooling anyone.

Comics provided me the comfort and strategy to cope with life until the truth finally became palatable, and I was strong enough to face the world and stop hiding. Was I conscious of this? No. But the superheroes gave me permission to protect myself. They gave me the strength to hide, as well as the rationale. Those stories fed my soul. They helped me defend myself and my secret life. For that, I will always be grateful. Comics offered me the script to remain safe until I could reveal my true identity when I was brave enough to live my life with no apologies.

When I faced my Kryptonite, I saw it for what it really was: a green rock from a made-up planet. I thank my superheroes for giving me that cover until I had enough inner strength to accept myself, come out of hiding, and live my life with no secrets.

WEEKEND AT BIG FOOT CABIN NEAR JEMEZ SPRINGS

JANET RUTH

Here on the side of a mountain, surrounded by women I've convened from times and places throughout six decades of life, we celebrate. We laugh and cry, tell stories of past escapades, and share sorrows—some past, some lingering. We watch snow sift down, reflect on family and friends, loss, and aging.

Playing games—old and new—*Clue* and *Quiddler*. We can't be bothered by competition, wink at inconvenient game rules, help each other win. Soaking in hot springs, we chuckle at sagging swimsuits.

wrinkled
goddesses
blue sky above steam

Painting our own wine glasses reveals hidden superpowers—both artists and those who profess an inability to draw stick figures. We produce—elegant gold leaves, sprigs of flowers, snowflakes, a whimsical armadillo, drifting blue dots, an orange octopus waving suckered arms.

With full glasses, we face—rental car stuck in snow down the hill, a sprained ankle, life's unexpected challenges revealed over green chile-chicken enchiladas. I face the trail up this inevitable mountain. From behind boulders and twisted tree roots emerge wonder women friends —no need for bustiers and capes, red boots, or those headbands with stars. They reach out and pull me up, shove me in the butt from behind, and link arms with me as we climb together.

60th birthday
I want to grow old
like a party

SUPERHERO SUNDAY IN OSAKA

SUZANNE KAMATA

When my twenty-three-year-old daughter Lilia, who is deaf, sent me a text saying she wanted to attend the Osaka Comic Convention, I messaged back, "Go ahead!" I assumed she would want to go with her friends, fellow manga and anime and Marvel movie enthusiasts. I am more of a literary novel-type person, unfamiliar with the DC universe. My idea of a good time is reading a book of poetry with a cat on my lap. However, a week or so later, she repeated her desire, along with a GIF of a crying cat, fountains of tears gushing from its eyes. This was followed by three attempted video phone calls while I was at work.

"Do you want me to go with you?" I texted.

"Yes," she replied.

Well, I could do this for her. On our mother-daughter trip to Paris several years back, she had put up with my dragging her (okay, pushing; she is a wheelchair user) to the Orsay Museum, even though she would have rather gone to the Concierge to look at a lock of Marie Antoinette's hair. She had made concessions for me so I could make some for her. Besides, I had never been to a comic convention before. It might be fun. At the very least, I could write about it.

I put her in charge of buying the tickets from the Japanese website.

She sent me a screenshot: 25,000 per ticket. What? "That's expensive," I texted her. "I'll pay for it," she texted back.

I later found out that admission was only 3,610 yen. The extravagant fees were for a photo opportunity with one of the celebrities headlining the event. One of them played the role of Lilia's favorite character in her favorite TV series. She had watched all ten episodes of all thirteen seasons and regularly posted related fan art on her Instagram feed. She had purchased the chance to be close to the actor.

Sure, it was expensive, but research has shown that experiences are often ultimately more satisfying than things. I know that to be true to myself. In Paris, we had a never-to-be-forgotten dinner at the top of the Eiffel Tower. When we went to Hawaii, on our last pre-pandemic trip, we had gone on an open-door helicopter ride. Having her photo taken with the celebrity would probably be just as thrilling for Lilia. She had also bought a ticket for me.

I didn't know much about the celebrity. In fact, I knew nothing. I had glimpsed him onscreen, occasionally, when Lilia was binge-watching episodes of the show on our widescreen TV. I looked him up on Wikipedia. He had an impressive background. He'd started out in politics, had probably met President Obama, and then transitioned into entertainment. He had kids, whom he was concerned about feeding well. Like me, his wife was a university professor, and he'd published a book of poetry, which I immediately ordered.

I started thinking about how I could make the most of this opportunity. As the author of several novels published by small presses, I always sought ways to promote my books. I knew that a celebrity endorsement – or even having a famous person be photographed while holding one's novel – could bring attention to a book. Maybe I could get the celebrity to hold my book during the photo-op, and then I could post it on Instagram.

But then I went to the website for the Comic Con. I came across a notice that one of the celebrities scheduled to appear in Tokyo in 2022 would not be coming after all. The message read, "Due to a last-minute personal issue," the celebrity "is unable to travel and had to postpone his appearance at this year's Tokyo Comic Con. He was looking forward to coming back to Japan and seeing everyone. He is deeply sorry and looks forward to returning to Japan next year." But the actor was not attending this year either. He had been run over by a snow plow a few months before and was still recovering. (This was not mentioned on the website.)

On the website, I came across a list of exhibitors, food vendors, celebrity guests (seven men, one woman), and rules regarding the autograph and photo sessions. There were so many rules! We would not be allowed to hug or touch the celebrities. We would not be allowed to take selfies or other photos with our smartphones, bring props (like a book?), wear masks, or give gifts to celebrities. Okay, so maybe I wouldn't be able to ask the TV star to hold my book.

Since the Comic Convention started relatively early, Lilia and I stayed overnight at a nice hotel in Osaka. The next morning, I put on make-up and a pretty dress. I helped Lilia with her hair. We went to the dining room for a gorgeous buffet breakfast – made-to-order omelets, tiny French pastries, a big bowl of fresh lychee fruits, and other delights. Although I had splurged on accommodations, I thought we would take public transportation to the convention site to save money. But that morning, on the third day of the event, the day of our scheduled photo op, rain poured down. We had forgotten to bring waterproof ponchos and umbrellas. I decided we'd go by taxi.

We hopped into a cab at the hotel. The driver was surprised when I mentioned the destination. "We'll have to go by highway," he said. That would mean toll fees. But at least we would get there on time and be relatively dry.

The venue, Intex Osaka, was over a bridge on a small island with many boxy warehouses. At first, I was amazed by the lack of cars. And people. Were we even in the right place? I didn't have enough cash for a taxi ride back to Osaka Station, and this driver didn't appear to take credit cards. At last, we reached the huge convention center.

"This is it!" the driver said. Still, no people. He continued to drive around the building, rain spattering his windshield, until, to my relief, we came across some men in uniform waving orange batons, and then to the front, where a long stream of young people holding umbrellas flowed toward the entrance.

Once inside, Lilia flashed our tickets. After a cursory bag check, red paper Comic Con bracelets were fastened to our wrists. I grabbed a map and tried to get my bearings, but Lilia whipped out her tablet, wrote something in Japanese, and showed it to one of the many attendants, a young man wearing a white surgical mask. She'd asked, "Where do we go for the celebrity photos?"

"I'll show you," the attendant said. "Follow me." We scurried past cosplayers dressed up like Spiderman and the Joker and one woman dressed in green carrying a huge candy cane. Some people, not in costume, were slurping noodles at a table near a food booth.

The attendant indicated an area at the back of the building. We still had a couple of hours before our photo session. "So, we just come here at one fifteen?" I asked. We had an appointment, after all.

"You should get here early," he said. "At least an hour before."

I nodded. "Now, where is the Celebrity Stage?"

According to the program, another actor, famous to this crowd, at least for his role in a movie based on an American comic book, would be participating in a Q and A session onstage in another twenty minutes. I figured we had plenty of time to find a good spot, but when we entered the enormous hall, I saw that all the seats were filled. We were late.

'This way," another attendant said, lifting the chain to the wheelchair-accessible area just to the left of the stage.

We had a good view, but I couldn't help thinking that at such an event in my native country, the United States, there would probably be a sign language interpreter. There was rarely one in Japan unless it was requested in advance. I did my best to interpret for my daughter.

In the program, the celebrity was pictured as bald and sleek. With his dark glasses, he appeared to be the epitome of cool. However, the man who ambled onto the stage looked a bit scruffy, as off-duty actors often do. He had a beard, glasses, and a leather newsboy cap over his frizzy grey hair. One of his teeth was missing. He greeted the crowd in Japanese and was met with applause.

The emcee tried to engage him in conversation, but he was hard to pin down. He wandered around the stage, joking around. When asked a fan's earnest question, "What special thing did you have to do to prepare for your role in the film?" he replied, "Nothing." Later, he was asked if he would appear in another superhero movie. He rubbed his fingers together to indicate it would depend on how much money he was offered, and then, to demonstrate how little most actors actually earn, he took out a one-thousand-yen bill and ripped a tiny corner off. I imagined the horror of the frugal, hard-working people in the audience who would never do such a thing. The emcee gently admonished him for tearing the money.

Finally, in true Japanese fashion, the emcee asked him to deliver a "special message" to his fans. The celebrity first avoided responding to the request, hopping off the stage and peering into the camera, pretending to check his teeth. Again, "A message for your fans, please?" He got back onstage and adjusted the interpreter's mic before, at last, delivering his "message," one Japanese word: "Hai."

In this country, where everyone was always so orderly and polite, I couldn't help but be embarrassed by his behavior. I wouldn't have attended a writer's festival or an academic conference without thinking about what I would say. Then again, maybe his performance – and he *was* performing – was better than him sitting calmly in the chair, giving straight answers. Maybe the unpredictability of this mad genius was entertaining. Maybe just seeing this man who had brought beloved characters to life onscreen, live and in-person, and to be able to pay homage to him was enough for his fans.

At about 12:10, after we checked out the exhibitors' tables and a display of manga posters, I suggested that we get in line for the photo session. Lilia eagerly rolled herself back to the spot we'd been shown to upon arrival. This time, we were early. Not only that, but we were also first in line. As we waited, Lilia composed a message to the celebrity on her smartphone. I figured that since she was deaf, the convention organizers would allow her to use her phone as a communication device.

A young woman in an orange kimono filed in behind us. More and more people followed. There were other cordoned-off rows for the other celebrities who would be signing autographs and posing for photos, including a Danish actor who was known for his role as a cannibal.

When we got closer to the appointment time, an attendant led us to another room, cordoned off like the immigration area of an international airport. Because my daughter uses a wheelchair, we had to take a shortcut. We were still at the head of the line. We were told to put all of our possessions into baskets – again, like the security line at the airport.

"My daughter is deaf," I explained. "Is it okay if she hangs on to her phone? She just wants to show a few words to the celebrity."

The attendant shook his head. "Talking to the celebrity is NG." No good. Prohibited.

Regretfully, I explained what he'd said to my daughter. Lilia, who had also read all the rules on the website, was nonchalant. She put her phone away without complaint.

We stood there, waiting. Although I had the addictive urge to check my email and scroll through social media, I left my phone in my bag. But I did reach for a notebook and pen.

"What are you doing?" my daughter asked.

"I'm just going to make a few notes," I told her. "I might write an essay about this."

"No, you can't write an essay." She made an "X" with her arms. No selfies, no touching the celebrity, no talking to the celebrity, and probably no writing about the celebrity.

"I think writing an essay is okay," I said. I scribbled a few words, then put the notebook and pen back into my bag.

I asked the attendant where the nearest subway or train station was, already thinking about how we would get home. My daughter asked me what we were talking about and then became irritated. I understood that she wanted me to focus on the celebrity, to think only about him and what would happen when he arrived. I tried.

More and more people, mostly Japanese women, lined up behind us. I began to realize why the organizers didn't allow conversation. If the celebrity had to engage in small talk with a hundred or more people, he would become exhausted. As it was, he'd have to smile non-stop for an hour or so. His cheeks would ache. But he would probably make a lot of money from doing this. I wondered how much of a cut he would get from the photo-op fees. I thought about all the times I had sat at a table in a bookstore or at a book festival, hoping to sell my novels, and no one had come. Yes, I envied the celebrity.

We waited and waited. The celebrity was late to the photo op. He was probably still signing autographs. Finally, we were led, just a few of us, including the young woman in the orange kimono, into a tented area with a backdrop. A photographer and team stood at the ready. My daughter began to tremble. She indicated that her heart was pounding: *doki doki*. I thought she was going to hyperventilate. We waited some more.

I wondered if this guy would be scruffy and irreverent like the actor onstage. I hoped not, for my daughter's sake. We had been planning to have our photo taken together, but at the last minute, Lilia changed her mind. She wanted to be in the photo alone with the celebrity. Fine with me.

"He's coming soon," someone said. "Please be patient."

And then…at last…he entered the tent. He was dressed nicely in a blue collared shirt and black pants, a bit of stubble peppering his handsome, now familiar face, his hair neatly groomed.

Lilia's hands flew to her flaming cheeks. She let out a squeal. Her extreme excitement amused the celebrity and everyone else. He smiled at her as she pulled up beside him in her wheelchair. A piece of tape served as a divider: fan on one side, celebrity on the other. He stood there towering over her with his aura of fame.

And then, Lilia's favorite actor, the man who brought her most beloved fictional character to life, crouched down so their heads were at the same level. He put his arm firmly around her shoulders. The woman behind me, no doubt as aware of the "no touching" rule as I was, gasped. The photographer clicked the shutter, and just like that, it was over. Lilia wheeled out of the way.

Next was my turn. I stepped up to the screen. The celebrity put his arm around me, and I smiled for the camera. "Thank you," I said in a low voice and exited the tent.

By the time we gathered our belongings, the photos were already printed and ready to be picked up. In the first one, Lilia and the celebrity grinned widely. She held both thumbs up. His body leaned toward hers. They both looked cute. In the second photo, my hands hung down, and my posture was stiff. The celebrity's smile was a tad dimmer, and….my eyes were closed.

But it was okay. The celebrity would probably never see this unflattering, awkward version of me or the hundreds of other photos taken at this and other Comic Cons. And at least I got an essay out of it. For my daughter, though, this had been the thrill of a lifetime. Expensive, yes, but more precious than gold.

Lilia fan art

Comic Con art display in Osaka with Lilia

Vendors at Comic Con

PART FOUR
ILLUSTRATIONS AND PHOTOGRAPHS

Colour My World

That I've waited to share
And dreams
Of our moments together
Colour my world with hope of loving you

- Chicago

SUPERNICK

FLOREN KUBAT

AVA'S ADVENTURES AT COMIC CON

AVA BRUNJES (AGE 8)

(New York City – October 2023)

My first day at Comic Con, I was pretty nervous. I was afraid people wouldn't like me because I was dressed as Darth Vader. He's a villain and uses the Dark Side of the Force. Godmama Goody (my godmother) reminded me that Darth Vader switched back to the Light Side in order to save Luke in *Return of the Jedi*. That made me feel better. My mom did my makeup that day for when I wanted to take off my helmet. It didn't look as good as I wanted it to.

I got to try on a real helmet from one of my favorite characters, Bo-Katan Kryze. It didn't really go with my Darth Vader costume, but I didn't care. I put my name in a raffle to win the helmet. I hope they pick me. I ask my mom every day to check her email to see if I won.

We went back to Comic Con a few days later. This time I was on fighting for the Light Side as Ahsoka Tano. Some other people were dressed like her, but the way she looks as a grown up from the new series. I wanted to look like her when she was in *The Clone Wars*. That's when she was younger, like me. Godmama Goody got me a makeup session with a professional at Comic Con so it looked really cool.

That is my mom next to me dressed as Peli Motto, the mechanic from *The Mandalorian*. We met tons of great people, and a bunch of them wanted to take pictures with us because they liked our costumes so much. I also went to Padawan Training to learn how to be a Jedi.

By the end of the second day, I wasn't nervous anymore.

Me (Ava Brunjes)

Me (without makeup and costume) with my godmother Gina Goodrowe, my mom's best friend since first grade. I call her "Godmama Goody" and she knows everything about Star Wars and got my mom and me into it.

PART FIVE
POETRY 2
WORDS

(Reprise)

It's only words,
and words are all I have
To steal your heart away.

- Bee Gees

STAN LEE, SOUTHWEST, AND SHAKESPEARE

STEVEN MICHAELS

Approaching 14,000 feet
her nervousness comes and goes
and I start thinking about Stan Lee.

Moments pass
my wife's head droops upon my shoulder
as our hands become more fastened
than our seatbelts
and I realize life's too short
to go it alone.

Suddenly
her head slides down a bit more
the air increasingly trembles.
If catastrophe should strike
we'd go out like Romeo and Juliet.
Or perhaps like Sue and Reed Richards
whose tragedy ended with superpowers.

I chuckle to myself
thinking how much Stan Lee
has become the new Shakespeare--
that *Two Gentlemen from Verona*
have been replaced by Thor and Captain America:
the singularity having something to do with capes.

At this altitude
It occurs to me how much the pen is my Mjolnir,
which, accompanied by her gentle breathing,
keeps me strong.

A sea of clouds bares us.
The seatbelt sign remains engaged.
Life no longer worries me:
here's to having lived it like
Stan, the Man, Lee.

THREE CEMENT MIXER OPERA

LINDA TROTT DICKMAN

(For the construction crew high atop Carnegie Hall)

It was the lone, long, lingering tone of the truck horn
that started it.
I heard Herb Alpert's "The Lonely Bull" in that one note,
The overture for

Cement mixer trio
Mixing
Mixing
Ever mixing

proceeding, ever gently
to music of Eric Korngold
for Robin Hood,
the love theme,
the Friar Tuck theme,
the triumphant hero theme.

At the street before Carnegie Hall
an octopus like cement pump
driving   pushing   elevating the cement
to a future rooftop garden setting.

Would they ever enter in?
Would those who sat in the new garden
Give any thought to the sweat, planning, time
that went into
a setting that after pouring will set,
cure over time
like fine music
then, all of a sudden, the theme from "Car Wash"
splashing all over the cement mixers
as they were readied for the next task.

Men singing duets
arias
solos
and finally
a chorus of cheers
as this new stage
takes form.
Work, and work

X-MEN

DAVION MOORE

We're all mutants
Unique creatures
With a special ability.
Wandering the world
That does not
Accept us
Freaks
Scary
Monsters
Hideous
Beasts
Strange
Odd
Peculiar
And other mean names
Are used to describe us
Yet they're mutants
Just like us
It is hard
To embrace your eccentricities

In a world that hates you
Is a challenge
But it is
A possibility
We struggle
But
We are
Who we are
And
Once you accept
Who you are
You become
Even stronger

TWO OLD GIANTS

LINDA DICKMAN

(For the twin oaks on Lancaster Rd., Clinton, MA)

They stood there, vibrant gray
Bound by hemp earrings
that held a throne.
We were propelled into the canopy,
pump by pump until dad
pushed, pushed us so high
he could fly under the swing
like Superman
and be back before we landed.

SAY "HELLO" AGAIN

MOLLY LIKOVICH

Was I there when Theseus became King of
Athens? When he breathed life into Olympia the way you breathed life
into me.

I read somewhere that he established The Cult of Aphrodite. Goddess
of love, painted in beautiful shades of scarlet.

Ariadne betrayed her father just to love him. I don't know who you
betrayed to love me. That knowledge, those memories, are sailing on
another ship somewhere, in an ocean I have
never seen.

Bones and blood. Wires and nerves. I am all these things you dreamed
me to be with scarlet-tipped fingers burning with a love that rips apart
the universe. With such ease. Like breakfast for dinner. Or an old song
from decades past. This—

"time-slice"

you've carved out for us, it is real. The river

of my mind, flows to the sea and my ship
is off its mooring—your scarlet-love is the
light guiding me safely back to shore.

I read it's bad luck to say goodbye in the dark. Or maybe I heard it in a
song. Or maybe I just wanted to see your face once more. I feel you.
Everywhere. In the bones I don't have and the memory of wires you
created and in the blood I'd gladly bleed for you if it meant we could
stay in this river—
always. We have said "goodbye" before,

so it stands to reason that we'll say "hello" again.

DAVION MOORE

Representation
Being seen
In ways unlike before
An authentic perspective
Showing the complexities
We all encounter in life
From Static shocking
To icon standing strong
To Rocket
To the Blood Syndicate
We're all together
Our differences make us stronger
And in this universe
We're striving for a better world

THE KING, THE PANTHER

DAVION MOORE

The king on his throne

Protecting the Wakandans

Hail King T'Challa

PART SIX
FICTION 2
HEROES AND VILLAINS IN THE NIGHT

"There are heroes and villains in the night,
Not obvious at first sight
Who's good?
Who's bad?
And who's just entirely insane"

"Heroes in the Night"

- Chris Delaney and the Brotherhood Blues Band

AN UNUSUAL VACATION

ROXANA NEGUȚ

"Though I walk through the valley of the shadow of death, I will fear no evil; for You are with me" Psalm 23.

Boston

Frederic had received the letter on a warm August afternoon. A large, thick envelope of luxury paper, gilded with gold letters and lacy edges, was waiting for him in the mailbox. The sender had written with capitalized letters: 'After Life,' one of Boston's largest insurance companies.

He vaguely remembered it; he contributed to them for a few years in his youth, and after that, he had given up. Occasionally, they sent him leaflets printed on glossy, colored paper, but over time, they also dwindled and disappeared.

The man opened the envelope only after going to the first floor. After an evening shower and the news he usually watched with a slight disinterest, he poured two fingers of whiskey into a glass and sat comfortably in the reading chair. He was not the curious type; another would have opened up from the first moments, but he wasn't that even in his youth, let alone in middle age.

His wife was the one who kept pushing him to do various social experiments, but after her death a few years ago, he didn't feel the slightest desire for something new. Indifference had gradually left its mark on his middle-aged face. So, he opened the envelope late in the evening, after two mouthfuls of whiskey, not very curious, not too impatient, as if it were an obligation he had to fulfill before going to bed.

He read, and for a few moments, he was taken by surprise, although this didn't happen to him very often. There, on the bold A4 sheet of paper, was written:

After Life Insurance Company is pleased to announce that you are the lucky winner of our raffle. You are one of the first customers of the company, since its establishment and on its 20th anniversary, there has been an anniversary raffle. The grand prize consists of a holiday in a luxury resort in the mountain resort of Sheol in the Alps. The holiday is for one person only, and it's not transferable during the Christmas holidays. The total value of the prize is $ 10,000, which includes the special treatment given to our winner. Please confirm your attendance during the selected period.

The surprised man read once more to make sure he understood correctly. Yes, Frederic Oxford's name was clearly written there, along with all his personal details. He was blown away; he had never won anything in his life. He didn't consider himself a lucky guy, and he hadn't heard from the company in years. However, there were only a few months until Christmas, and he had no special plans. There was nothing on the horizon.

In recent years, he had spent his holidays alone. The same dull ritual was celebrated yearly: a turkey breaded in the oven, a good movie, and sleep. He sometimes lacked the patience for his relative's phone calls. Two years ago, when his brother announced his visit with his wife and two teenage children were going to visit, he politely refused him on the pretext of leaving the country. An urgent delegation that he could not refuse in any way. Frederic knew that was lonely, but his daily social contact and hours of work were enough.

He had a team to prepare. He was the head of a cigarette sales department, and the daily tasks were many and demanding. He had progressed over the years. A young man full of hope and zeal had been employed there as a courier at the cigarette company in his youth, and now, twenty years later, he had become the head of an entire department.

He studied all the data in the letter once again. He had nothing planned for Christmas and thought that the air of the mountain resort and the novelty of the place would revive him a little. He had never traveled to Europe before. So, he decided to accept. With all his characteristic reserve, he felt it was an irrefutable offer. *Oh, Amanda would have loved it!* he thought.

She was so adventurous; she loved to travel to live every moment to the fullest. Too bad the disease pushed her so young into the arms of death. He didn't even know she was sick. She came home from work one evening a little pale and more tired. She complained about feeling pain in her chest, but she had it before and didn't care too much about it. But, on that warm August night, his delicate wife, Amanda, died. A cardiac arrest knocked her down at just 37 years old.

Three years had passed since then, but Frederic could not yet understand the speed of death over life. Just a few minutes, and you're done. This was the difference between life and death.

They didn't have any children, so he was left alone at the age of 42, overwhelmed with loneliness and pain. He left for work in the morning and returned late in the evening, a routine in which every day was the same. Yes, this holiday was exactly what he needed. Something to get him out of the black abyss of habit he'd been in after Amanda's death.

The next day, he called the company's headquarters and confirmed acceptance of the award. The voice at the other end of the line, kind and warm, a young woman's voice lightly interrogated him, asking for more data and then promising him an unforgettable experience.

The months passed quickly, one after the other, and a few days before Christmas, Frederic prepared for the journey.

He bought some thick new clothes adapted for the mountains. He cut his blond hair that exceeded a decent limit and announced to the doorman of the block where he lived that he would be gone for a week. He left him the key to water the pants, telling him about the holiday at the same time. The nice old man was also amazed by the luck that befallen Frederic and congratulated him from the bottom of his heart. The doorman felt terrible about the loss of Frederic's wife. He had liked the pretty, kind lady on the fourth floor, and he was moved by the tragedy the poor man had gone through.

A few hours after leaving the house, Frederic boarded the plane. He was in business class and had many hours of flying to the Alps. Along the way, he befriended a fellow passenger. He told him about the raffle, but Sam, a businessman who had traveled the world, hadn't heard anything about the small, unknown mountain resort.

The truth was that Frederic hadn't found it either, though he looked for the resort on the maps. However, the leaflets received in the envelope convinced him. The luxury cottage and the mountain scenery looked like fairy tales. Additionally, according to the schedule, a limousine would pick him up from the airport, so he didn't have to worry too much about the route.

The flight went smoothly, and when he reached his destination, Frederic said goodbye to Sam with the promise that they would meet for a beer in the middle of summer when he passed through Boston.

After the plane landed at the small Alpine airport, he saw the limousine. He didn't ask anyone; the people around him spoke French, and Frederic could barely handle a few common phrases. However, the company assured him that the cabin staff spoke English so he would have no communication problems. The limousine was waiting for him with the same capital, glossy letters After Life, and the driver, a young man, weak and pale as wax, spoke to him in broken English and told him they would arrive at the cottage in just a few hours.

On the way, Frederic admired the scenery, poured himself a glass of champagne, and finally relaxed. The cold weather and heavy snow took him by surprise. He wasn't accustomed to such low temperatures.

In Boston, the winter was warmer, and in recent years, they didn't have an ounce of snow. But here, the scenery was truly spectacular. The old snow-covered fir trees lined the narrow road on which the car was moving. The mountains loomed in the sky in an unusual color, far too dark, and the snow was like in fairy tales. It was the perfect setting for the winter holidays. At one point, the limousine made a detour, slowed down, and entered a forest, and the surrounding landscape changed dramatically. The road turned into a narrow path, surrounded by strange-shaped trees, which Frederic had never seen before. Looking closely, he saw ghostly figures over two meters high, like dark forest guards. The sky also changed its color dramatically, and in some parts, it looked broken, perforated, and repaired here and there with patches of black, like a gloomy, old, scary picture forgotten above the forest.

When it was already dark outside, the limousine stopped in front of a cottage. Surrounded by a thick, blunt stone fence, the house had a strange architecture that seemed detached from long ago. Moreover, the fog that surrounded it and which settled into the woods didn't help by offering a very welcoming air.

"Here it is, sir, the cottage where you will spend your vacation,' the driver told him. "Welcome to Sheol!" He showed him the narrow road that led to the gate of the house.

Frederic took his trolley from the car's trunk, but he didn't have the chance to say anything to the driver because he left in a whirlwind, as if he had been chased by an unseen enemy. In just a few minutes, the car disappeared down the narrow path as if it turned invisible.

The stone cottage was inscribed with the same bold gold letters as on the car, *After Life,* and the resort's name, *Sheol.* The letters shone brightly in the dim light of the evening as if engulfed in flames. But it was already getting dark outside, and Frederic told himself he might be a little tired, and his blurred vision played tricks on him.

As he entered the cottage, the old iron door creaked strangely like a child's cry and opened with great difficulty. He descended a few steps on a rather narrow staircase and found himself in a huge hall with dark paneling, dark furniture, and thick carpets inscribed with Egyptian hieroglyphs that reigned everywhere. The smell inside was different from anything he had ever encountered: a heavy scent of incense mixed with fir and old wood in the air.

At the small oval reception desk made of solid, lacquered wood, a pale, thin young man sat, and Frederic was surprised to find that he looked strikingly like the limousine driver. You'd think they were twin brothers. He handed him a note from the owner of the cottage.

'Welcome, Mr. Oxford! We wish you a pleasant stay, and please enjoy the unique holiday entertainment just for you. You are our only guest during this period. However, before you enjoy your vacation, we also have some requirements.

All personal belongings, cards, ID, and telephone will be left in the reception safe. Each day, you must complete a questionnaire with questions about yourself. Our holidays are personalized, and we want to get to know you better. We promise you an unforgettable experience!

Frederic thought these requirements seemed a little strange and told himself that this must be the custom there and handed over his personal belongings to the reception safe, receiving a small, golden key to access the safe.

The landlord handed him the daily form, telling him in the same broken English and hoarse, slightly hollow voice, "Complete it, and after that, you can enjoy your first holiday evening in peace."

When Frederic opened the form, there was only one question printed in large, bold letters in the middle of the sheet: *Do you regret it?* Next to it was printed on white paper a colorful nightmare scene: a motorcycle and a man lying on the wet asphalt. There was blood, a great deal of blood.

Unable to believe his eyes, Frederic looked at the printed scene once more. In his mind, shock and fear gradually set in. *How did they know?* He wondered. Only Amanda knew, and she died just like the young man on the road. It was the sin of his youth. The day that changed him forever.

He had barely gotten his motorcycle license, was young and defiant, climbed up the bike after drinking, and had taken a curve too fast and hit a pedestrian. He was so frightened that he fled the scene of the accident and a few days later heard in the news report that the young man had died at the hospital. Since then, remorse has not given him peace. Maybe if he hadn't drunk a few beers, he would have been more careful. Perhaps if he stopped for the young man and helped him by giving first aid, he would have lived. However, he never thought he would become a killer with a momentary mistake. It was the burden of his life. Police never caught him, and the young man's death was later classified as an accident by an unknown perpetrator. He never had the courage to surrender.

As the years passed, Frederick knew that his heavy conscience, fear, and regret would torment him all his life. So, he wrote on the questionnaire as a first and sincere confession:

YES, in large, bold letters and trembling hands. He left the questionnaire at the front desk.

The quiet young man took the questionnaire and handed him the key to his room. When he left, Frederic rubbed his eyes, and it seemed to him in a flash that the young man was wearing a pair of hooves that appeared to be sticking out from under his black suit with a whip and too-long pants.

He went upstairs to the two floors and opened the door to his room. 31/07 was written in gold letters on the wooden door. It was the date of the accident, printed on the door of his room.

But when he stepped inside, after only a few steps, he woke up outside his room. Under his astonished gaze, the same nightmare scene unfolded on the crash road, and from there, as a witness, he watched the whole scene again from the beginning. He saw himself, a young man in a leather jacket and a powerful engine, approaching the curve with his motorcycle, and then he saw the young teenager preparing to cross the road. Inattentively, he was looking for something in the backpack he was holding in one of his hands. A few more steps, and he would have lost his life. At the last moment, Frederic jumped and pulled him off the side of the road, pushing him with an invisible push. The motorcycle passed, and the young man who had fallen on the asphalt looked around, puzzled. There was no one around him, as if he had suddenly stopped.

But Frederic couldn't do anything; after a split second, he was back in his room in the cottage. Dizzy, disoriented, and especially bounded by an endless fatigue.

He lay down on the large wooden bed, dazed by his experience. He fell into a deep sleep…hours of sleep that promised to heal him of the scene he had just relived.

When he woke up, Amanda was standing a few steps away from him. She looked at him with a smile of gratitude in her bright eyes, but after only a few moments, the woman disappeared— a mirage of just a few seconds.

What kind of strange place was this? Frederic wondered. A place where you could travel in the past and meet the dead? Nobody would believe him. He had to know if he was whole-minded or if all this was just a figment of his imagination. He jumped out of bed and sat down at the small antique desk in the room, on the surface of a small, modern silver laptop. He had seen it since last night, but his experience had distressed him, and he had no desire for anything else.

He typed on the keyboard, Arvin Maiker… and the search engine showed him dozens of images with the young man. He was a world athlete and had won several international competitions. In all the pictures, he was overwhelmed with medals and smiled happily.

The young man was alive now, Frederic thought, and breathed a sigh of relief, though he knew there was no logical explanation for what had just happened. But for the first time in many years, he felt a huge weight lifted from his shoulders.

And suddenly, he sensed this place might hold other surprises for him. But although scared, he did not want to leave. Something that seemed above his powers attracted and kept him here. Maybe he'll see Amanda again…to apologize. She hadn't known that the soothing sedative he had given her in the last few weeks of her life brought her death. Her heart was too fragile. Amanda had insisted that he should go and surrender to the police, but Frederic was a coward. His whole life would have been destroyed in an instant. He would have ended up behind bars, and, in addition, the young man on the motorcycle would not have been revived by that gesture. But Amanda didn't understand, and to calm her panic attacks, he had brought her that soothing seda-tive. It was not recommended for cardiac patients. Neither he nor

Amanda had known this fact, and this brought such an abrupt end to his wife's life.

The man was interrupted by his dark thoughts and regrets by a knock on the door.

'I brought you breakfast,' the waiter told him.

Frederic studied the food carefully; this was his favorite food from childhood, which he hadn't seen for decades. It was also Amanda's favorite dessert, burnt sugar cream. It was like a divine sign. He sat down and ate quietly; nothing surprised him anymore.

After breakfast, he went down to the reception, but instead of yesterday's young man, there was another man, but he also looked strikingly like the others, only an older version.

"I'm Frederic Oxford, and I'd like my daily questionnaire."

All the while, he studied himself in the front desk mirror; his hair was a little thinner, and it turned a bit grayer. The wrinkles on his forehead and cheeks were much more pronounced, as if five or six years had passed, not just one night. He had suddenly aged.

The man at the front desk handed him the questionnaire with a smile. When he opened the envelope, Frederic saw Amanda's picture beside him, and on the bottom half of the sheet was a picture of himself lying in bed in his Boston apartment. The old man in the apartment was about to die. Somewhere in the corner, a candle was burning. Frederic felt the weight of the words printed on the sheet of paper. *Check the selected image. That's how it was written there.*

He took the pen and, with a trembling heart, ticked off Amanda's image. He would have chosen her a thousand times.

' "Very well, Mr. Frederic," said the receptionist, smiling.

He suddenly felt tired, so tired that he wanted to lie on the thick carpet in the lobby of the cottage to sleep.

"I'll go upstairs for a few moments," he told the receptionist.

In the elevator mirror, he looked frightened, as if ten more years had passed. Just like that, in an instant. He didn't know, and he didn't seem to want to know what kind of place he was in. Time was running out so fast. And besides, it was always night outside. The night, the forest, and the snow, just that. He would have asked the receptionist several times, but he wanted to avoid talking with the strange man.

Who knows what answers he would receive, and he wasn't sure he wanted to hear them.

He reached his room, and there he saw the same image again. Amanda was waiting for him, smiling. She whispered, "I forgive you!" and pointed with her hand.

On the opposite wall of the room, two doors had opened, one showing his living room in Boston. Amanda appeared again at the other door, smiling. She held out her hand. Frederic chose. He knew what would happen to him if he chose the Boston door.

He walked to the other door and took his wife by the hand. His place was next to her. Life for life, he thought, because he finally understood. If he had returned to Boston, everything would have returned to normal, and Alvin Meiker would have remained an unsolved case, a tragic death.

The next morning, when the room-service boy entered the empty room, all that was left of Frederic was lying on the thick carpet – his watch, clothes, shoes, and a small pile of ashes.

The boy packed them all in a bag labeled *After Life* and sent them to the owner of the insurance company. Another case was resolved.

Downstairs at the front desk, the man opened the thick black register, cut out Frederic's name, and began to study the next case...Sam, the businessman. Eventually, it was everyone's turn to pay for their sins.

Sheol, a hell-like underground place. The Assyrians, Babylonians, and Jews believed it to be the abode of souls after death until the final judgment.

IN THE LONG RUN

WILLIAM JOHN ROSTRON

"When it all comes down,
We will still come through,
in the long run."

- The Eagles

"Anna, I'm doing it…just like you wanted me to. This one last time is for you," Jimmy mumbled as he prepared for the starter's gun. It had been a long battle to get here—both emotionally and physically. He had been in his fifties when he started taking running seriously. That seemed kind of late, but when people commented, he glibly replied, "Better late than never."

By the time he hit sixty, he had already run three New York City Marathons and had no plans of stopping his annual tradition—until tragedy struck. Anna's breast cancer had at first seemed curable, but that proved a mirage. From her first diagnosis to her tragic death, it had been a decade of false hope and bad news. Jimmy hadn't had the time to run, even though he knew that doing so would relieve some of the pressure and anxiety he felt. He would not leave Anna's side long enough to train sufficiently for a 26.2-mile race.

Then she passed. However, in one of their many deathbed conversations, she insisted—no demanded, that he get right back in the groove and run again.

"Do it for me," she had rasped with a voice that she knew was limited. Jimmy had mourned her inconsolably. They had been childhood sweethearts, high school sweethearts, college sweethearts, and then they had married. Unable to have children, it had been only the two of them for more than five decades of their lives. Now that he was alone, his running consumed him. It somehow made him feel that Anna was with him. He was doing it for her. He had cried even as he put on his shorts and laced his sneakers for the first time in ten years. Eventually, however, the runners' high that enveloped him each training session became his way of thinking of Anna—of being with her.

He ran every day, no matter what the outside weather. He ran every day, no matter his condition. His heart almost exploded on many occasions, and he wondered if it was the strain of his activity at an advanced age or whether he was feeling the effects of a truly broken heart. And now he was here at the starting line of the marathon. Though the front of his shirt was black except for his pinned running number, the back had the two words that he had had a tailor embroidered on it—*For Anna.*

"Anna, it's started. There's the gun, and we are now entering the lower level of the Verrazzano Bridge. Remember, I told you about the 'sound wave?' Well, it's beginning. The sound begins with the cheering at one end of the almost mile-long span and weaves its way until it arrives at the other end. It is something that only those involved in it can experience. But I wanted to share it with you."

Jimmy realized that his legs were churning at a speed way too fast. He knew that was created by the excitement of finally being here again —and doing it for Anna. However, if he kept up this pace, he would begin to run anaerobically, preventing him from finishing the race. He would not stop, but he could slow down and figuratively smell the roses.

Passing through various ethnic neighborhoods in Brooklyn brought back many memories—beautiful memories of time spent with his life-long love—all the romantic dinner experiences with Middle Eastern, Hispanic, and Asian food that they so enjoyed. The miles flew by as he was lost in many wonderful memories. And then, he came to the 59th Street Bridge.

This East River crossing made famous by Simon and Garfunkel for its hook line, "Feelin' groovy," engendered the exact opposite reaction in Jimmy. His run across this bridge plunged him into the depression of Anna's struggle. For ten years, this bridge had been their path to Memorial Sloan-Kettering Cancer Center. And now, he journeyed the entire length of the span with tears in his eyes.

"I miss you, Anna," whispered Jimmy as he exited the bridge ramp that funneled him onto 1st Avenue on the island of Manhattan. There, his mood was lifted by the crowds of onlookers who stood three deep and cheered even the slowest of runners. Anna had been in that crowd every time he ran this marathon. She had stood in the same spot every year and provided him with a bottle of water and an inspirational kiss. He looked to her usual location, and his eyes betrayed him into thinking she was there. As he started to veer to the crowd, he was filled with anticipation—until the illusion disappeared. He kept running.

In Harlem, scores of boom boxes blared festive music as the crowds encouraged runners to "move their feet" or "do their thing." Thanks to this boisterous support, he got his second wind just as he approached "the wall." This moment in every runner's marathon signifies the time when it seems prudent to give up. It is when all physical resources are drained, and it is only by the force of will the runner can continue. The wall consumed Jimmy just as he returned to Manhattan from a brief run through the Bronx.

At this point, he was barely running—his feet going through the motions that would propel him ever so slightly forward. Dehydration was stalled only by the offers of water by volunteers along the route. His mind began to blur, and he saw nothing but the few steps ahead of him.

"Anna, I will make it—I promised you...," Jimmy murmured only to himself. "I promise." The outer edge of Central Park now came into view. This meant he only had two more miles--two very long miles. He saw nothing. He felt nothing. Only the vision of Anna kept him going.

He traveled along the park from its northernmost border to its southern edge. There, he turned the corner and saw the balloons that signified the gateway to the finish line. He cursed the fact that the official marathon a century before had been lengthened by .2 of a mile. This change accommodated the English royal family's children's desire to see the Olympic starting line. *Damn those kids* was all he could think.

He was so close he could almost touch the finish line—and he would in seconds. His heart felt like it would burst, and he put on a final acceleration of speed. With every joint throbbing with pain, he began to feel no one ache in particular. He reached out with his hand as if the few extra inches it provided would hasten his finish. He saw his feet cross the line almost simultaneously with his total collapse.

"Anna, I made it…for you."

"You know I only encouraged you so that it would take your mind off of me," answered Anna.

"If that is the case, it didn't work," Jimmy answered. "All I could think of was you…and how I wanted to be with you."

"You are."

"What's that mean?"

"You are with me…now…and forever."

"Forever?"

"Forever."

"Did you ever see anything like this before?" remarked the assistant EMT after exhausting every life-saving technique he knew.

"No, he finishes the whole marathon, and then…" replied his boss.

"Yeah, and I can't understand…"

"The smile on his face?"

"I guess he died happy…you know, finishing the marathon."

With that, the medical team lifted the body onto the gurney. In the process, they turned Jimmy over and saw the words on the back of the tee shirt—*For Anna.*

"No, I don't know why, but I just get the feeling that it was something bigger than the race…something much bigger."

THE CLOCK

ROXANA NEGUT

In the small American town of Greenwich, Connecticut, every day, everything was about the same. People were born, lived, and died in the same daily routine without a single thing disturbing them. An outside observer would have said that nothing out of the ordinary ever happens in the small town, but things were not quite like that.

Each year, at the end of October, more precisely on the last day of the month, all the clocks in the city stopped. Only one still ticked, but its loud sound covered all, for it was the ticking of death. The house where it was heard was also the one where the tenant lost his life. This was the city's dark secret, the curse of the clock, as they called it.

No one knew how it appeared at first; in the first fifty years, no one gave it much importance, but one day, a sheriff noticed that it was something unusual. Finch, the sheriff, began to follow the signs over time and discovered more bizarre coincidences. No one knew how the clock chose the next victim. But the beatings were the same, seven each time, and then the unfortunate man's life ended suddenly.

When they learned the sheriff's theory, the frightened townspeople tried to escape. Some threw away all the clocks from their homes, hoping to delay the moment, but in vain. Others left the city, but the cursed ticking followed them everywhere. One thing was for certain: if you were born in Greenwich, there was no escaping the curse.

Finch, the impressed sheriff by the fate of the people, tried for more than twenty years to find a solution. For several years in a row, he prepared doctors to revive the chosen one of the clocks immediately, but in vain. At one of these annually organized meetings, Allen, the mayor's councilor, and mathematics teacher, passionate about quantum physics and mysteries, proposed an original thing: that all the inhabitants should try to fool the clock by one day, the fateful day. Thus, he said, they would skip the last day of October, going directly into the next calendar month, November. No anniversaries, no parties, more than that, those born on that day will be registered in the following month; practically, the last day of October will be permanently erased from their calendar and life.

The solution, although original, did not work. That year, the clock took Louise, the town's new librarian. Only then did the townspeople realize that the clock cannot be fooled.

They made peace with the idea, and year after year, they fell mowing from the fatal ticking. One good thing in all the drama was that they learned to live each moment and enjoy it as if it were their last. For some of them, it really was.

Until one day, when Jeremy Lock returned to the small town, Jeremy had left the city as a child and, together with his parents, famous archaeologists, had visited worldwide. He had seen all the continents, but the terror in his parents' eyes was the same whenever October 31 came. When Jeremy turned 19, the clock's ticking caught him in India. There, an old shaman, hearing his story, advised him what to do. The old man told him that the clock came from another world, another dimension, and there, it was something natural, A good of nature, but once a year, he wandered from his timeline and hit the ground in our time and universe.

Therefore, Jeremy returned to Greenwich, determined to stop the cycle before it was too late. He gathered the bravest people in the city, and they began to search for the portal to another world. Night after night, they roamed the woods surrounding the city with the energy detectors. From the shaman's information, the place the clock was coming from had an energy of over 700 HZ on the Hawkins scale, which was the most important clue.

They kept walking until they reached the scariest area on the western edge of the city. The forest was nicknamed for hundreds of years, Shelter of the Unclean', and an old local legend told that the souls of those who died there changed into trees.

The five people on the team reached an area he called Active Energy Point 2.

It wasn't until the fourth night of their search that they discovered the portal, a narrow cave in the forest's heart. It was an unusual area —Earth's heart. The team consisted of Jeremy, who led the whole expedition, Dr. March, Finch, the sheriff, the forester, and Cathy, the only woman in the group.

Only Jeremy and Cathy entered, but before they could take a few steps, the mouth of the tunnel suddenly opened, leaving them trapped underground. And they continued on their way, and the ancient tunnel widened as they advanced. After a while, whether it was a good few minutes or hours, it was hard to say because time seemed to flow differently here. The tunnel bifurcated, and the two, guided by the strange light on the walls, turned left to the area that shone the brightest. They knew they didn't have much time left.

When only a few seconds passed after seven o'clock, the clock materialized in front of them; it seemed made of shadows and light, fog, empty areas, a bizarre mirror on which the numbers could be seen, a shiny projection whose reflections opened dozens of doors around. Frozen, the two did not know precisely how to proceed; they had never seen anything like it before, but Jeremy took out of his backpack the last remnants of osmium, the rarest metal on earth, obtained with the approval of the mayor from the city's treasury. They were the last remains of a meteorite that had fallen to earth decades ago.

On the 6th beat, Jeremy put the strange, heavy metal from his hand into the heart of the clock. And suddenly, dozens of flashes gathered in the room, chaotic bursts of light alternating with shadows. Only then did the clock stop ticking, and after that, in a few minutes, it completely dematerialized as if it was never there. Silence and darkness fell in the tunnel.

Months passed quickly, one after the other, and the townspeople freed from the curse were happier than ever. They had even decided that the end of October would be Greenwich Town Day, like a second revival.

On the last day of October, the first year without the watch, Jeremy felt strange. His heart was pounding for no reason, strong palpitations; with the sides of his eyes, he saw trembling shadows that seemed to accompany him everywhere.

A dream that the next day became real. On the last day of October, in the evening, while Jeremy's heart was beating violently with fibrillation, for the seventh time at the fixed hour, Sheriff Finch's heart suddenly stopped, and he fell to the ground. He was the last person Jeremy had spoken to.

Only then did Jeremy realize he had turned into the city's cursed clock.

JUST A SONG BEFORE I GO

EDITOR'S FINAL THOUGHTS

KAPOW was a huge undertaking. What started as a small poetry book centering on superheroes, soon became what you see before you…an all-inclusive book with multiple forms of expression. This was a new direction for Red Penguin Books, and we would like to hear what you, the reader, think. What worked and what didn't work. What pieces hit the mark…and which did not? Did you like how it was set up? Was any story, poem, or nonfiction piece too long? Too short?

As Santayana wrote, "Those who forget the past are doomed to repeat it." We would like to move on to bigger and better anthologies using our past as an educational tool. Please help us do that.

Email: William John Rostron at BandintheWind@gmail.com

Please put KAPOW as you message title. Thank you.

Our contributors ranged from a young girl who just turned eight to authors closing in on eighty.

MEET THE EDITOR

William John Rostron's books have a readership that spans four continents and all fifty states. His series of novels steeped in the 1960s music and culture, Band in the Wind, Sound of Redemption, and Brotherhood of Forever, have received critical acclaim from Writers Digest, the Online Book Club Review, and have consistently received Amazon ratings of 4.5 out of 5, or higher. He recently added to this series with The Other Side of the Wind, a book that may be read either independently of the series or in addition to it. He has published over three dozen short stories in anthologies, five receiving awards from Writers Digest in 2022. Many of these pieces appear in his short story compilation, A Flamingo Under the Carousel. Five of his stories s have been produced on the New York stage and are available for viewing on the author's website. Recently, he has finished work editing the Red Penguin anthology, KAPOW. www.WilliamJohnRostron.com

Born and raised in Queens, NY, William John Rostron now splits his time between his home on Long Island and traveling the country in his Tiffin motorhome. He is busy completing a bucket list of travel adventures when not writing. In the past 18 years, he and his wife, Marilyn, have traveled 140,000 miles. These journeys have taken them to the 48 contiguous states, 133 national parks, all 30 major league baseball stadiums, 154 cities and towns, two Canadian provinces, and various unusual experiences and locations. Many of these locations have served as backgrounds for his books.

He is presently working on a second book of short stories tentatively titled T-Rex Stole My Computer and a fifth novel, Dancing with the Lost.

www.WilliamJohnRostron.com

MEET OUR CONTRIBUTORS

Ava Marie Brunjes is a 3rd grade student in Sawmill Elementary School in North Bellmore. She enjoys dressing up as Star Wars characters, Disney villains, and pirates. She recently earned her red belt in Taikwondo.

Linda Trott Dickman–award winning poet, author of four chapbooks, a book of poetry prompts called *Catching the Light- Poetry Prompts for Children of All Ages*. Her work has been nationally and internationally anthologized . She is the coordinator of poetry for the Northport Arts Coalition, teaches at the Walt Whitman Birthplace, Northport Historical Society and at Samantha's Li'l Bit O' Heaven. Linda was chosen as a New York State Woman of Distinction in 2023.

Eric Esquivel is a top-secret science experiment from Los Angeles, California. His government-issued cybernetic heart pumps blood that has been tainted by the bite of a radioactive spider. His strange and terrible powers are fueled by his exposure to Earth's yellow sun.

His previous clients include: Archie Comics, Boom Studios, DC, Dynamite, Heavy Metal Magazine, IDW, National Hispanic Media Coalition, Papercutz, Scholastic, Spookshow Records, Starlite Pulp, TidalWave Productions, Vertigo, and Zenescope.

Alex Grehy loves to write relatable pieces that engage the reader's emotions and helps them to make sense of the world around them. Her work has been published in a range of anthologies and ezines worldwide including Gnashing Teeth Publishing and Red Penguin Collections. Her work is also available via a global network of prose & poetry dispensers run by French publisher, Short Edition. Alex's sweet life is filled with narrowboating, rescue greyhounds, singing and chocolate, a sound foundation for her original view of the world, expressed in vivid prose and thought-provoking poetry.

Suzanne Kamata is an American permanent resident of Japan. She is the author or editor of several published books including the young adult novel GADGET GIRL: THE ART OF BEING INVISIBLE, which features manga artist Aiko Cassidy, creator of a female superhero; the award-winning memoir SQUEAKY WHEELS: TRAVELS WITH MY DAUGHTER BY TRAIN, PLANE, METRO, TUK-TUK AND WHEELCHAIR; and the adult novel THE BASEBALL WIDOW, which was selected International Book of the Year by the Pulpwood Queens and Timber Guys Book Club. She has an MFA from the University of British Columbia and is an associate professor at Naruto University.

Hello! My name is Floren Kubat, I am a non-binary argentinian freelance illustration artist (uff, that was long). I have been struggling with the portrayal of my art, I started with film making and then with writting and then with drawing and now, now I am mixing all up in a blender and expect for the best.

You figure it out, I am a massive geek and nerd, a fan of our lord Nicolas Cage and I am NOT a fan of foot. Over and out.

Molly Likovich holds a Bachelor's Degree in Creative Writing from Salisbury University. She's the Bestselling Author of the romance novella 'Riding The Headless Horseman' she also penned the titles 'Send in The Clowns', and 'Loved Alone ' amongst others. She is also the co-author of the poetry collections 'Not a Myth' and 'The Willow's Silence'. Her individual poems and short stories have appeared in numerous magazines and journals including Rust + Moth, Shore Poetry, and The New Mexico Review, among others. In 2023 she won Second Place in the Auvert Magazine Orange Skies Poetry Contest and was a Finalist in The Nation's National Amateur Poetry Competition.

Born in Atenas, Costa Rica, 1969, Henry Vinicio Valerio Madriz graduated in English Teaching and Linguistics & Literature. Photography lover. He's published "Strange Fate," "Darkness Falls," "Loving Shadows," "Dear You," The Red Penguin, USA; "Running", Strangest Fiction Volume One, USA; "The Cyrenian", Otherwise Engaged Literature and Arts Journal Volume 11, USA; "My Love's Gone On A Train" and "Treasure," Younker! The Flight Of Youthful Temptations, India; and "Green Mirrors," All Your Stories, December 2023, UK. He got shortlisted with his poem "Soldiers' Death Sentence" in Voice of Peace: 1st Intercontinental Poetry And Short Story Anthology 2021, The League of Poets.

Steven Michaels is the pen name of teacher Steve Piscitello, whose students at Winchester School in New Hampshire helped create the plot for the skit featured in this anthology. He is also the author of Sweet Life of Mystery, a spoof of the whodunnit genre. Lastly, he is the co-founder of Quabbin Quills, a nonprofit writing group that publishes anthologies for New England writers and scholarship winners from area teens and college age students. Visit quabbinquills.org for more details.

Davion Moore is an Ohio writer that loves sports, comic books and video games. He recently received his master's degree in Sports Journalism from St. Bonaventure University.

Roxana Neguț is a poet, writer, and journalist from Bucharest, Romania, born in 1981. She pursued her education in Philosophy and Journalism at the University and gained experience working as an editor, copywriter, content writer, and journalist for various publications. Roxana Neguț has an impressive portfolio of writing, including children's literature books, short stories, poetry books, and her writing have been published in national and international literary magazines and anthologies.

Her writing has earned her several awards, such as the "Ambassador of the word," the "Friendship Award for a Story" in the International Contest Univers XXL, the "Short Story Contest – Paranormal" Incorporated by 4 Horsemen Publishing SUA, "The Iconic Author Award" by Maybeify Publisher -India.

Author site :https://roxananegut.com

Robert Primavera wrote original superhero stories at age 12. His partner in this endeavor six decades ago was Kapow editor William John Rostron.

Janet Ruth is a NM ornithologist. Her writing focuses on connections to the natural world. Recent poems in Tiny Seed Literary Journal, Tulip Tree Review, Ocotillo Review, Ekphrastic Review, and anthologies including Unknotting the Line: the Poetry in Prose (Dos Gatos Press, 2023). Her sonnet "A World That Shimmers" won the inaugural True

Concord Poetry Contest, was set to music by the 2023 Stephen Paulus Emerging Composer and performed by True Concord Voices & Orchestra in Tucson (October). Her book, Feathered Dreams: celebrating birds in poems, stories & images (Mercury HeartLink, 2018) was a NM/AZ Book Awards Finalist. https://redstartsandravens.com/janets-poetry/

Bea Sage is actually three writers stacked on top of each other wearing a trenchcoat. Together, they have stories in publications including Red Penguin's 'A Heart Full of Love' and 'Stand Out: Vol 1', '72 Hours of Insanity: Writer's Games' Vol. 7, 9, & 10, TL;DR Press's 'Breathless', online at Little Old Lady Comedy, Defenestration, and Bullshit Lit, and have placed in the Writer's Workout 'Writer's Games' for three consecutive years. One or the other of them can usually be found ignoring the advice of the other two and buying more books and/or mugs and/or sweaters.

Carmen White is a writer who spent her childhood falling off horses and raising baby goats.

Carmen studied Creative Writing at BYU-Idaho and writes books about her many adventures—be it real life or imaginary.

She now lives in North Carolina where she's raising two more outdoor loving/bookworm hybrids just like herself.

ALSO FROM THE RED PENGUIN COLLECTION

FICTION

What Lies Beyond – Sci-Fi Stories of the Future

I Can't Find My Flashlight – Contemporary Campfire Stories

A Heart Full of Love – A Collection of Romantic Short Stories

Behind Closed Doors – A Mystery Anthology

Once Upon A Time… – A Fairy Tale Anthology

Ernest Lived …and other Historical Fiction Short Stories

Until Dawn – A Supernatural Anthology

Treat-or-Trick – Halloween Horror Stories

Pets On the Prowl – An Animal Mystery Anthology

My Robot & Me – A Not-So Fiction Anthology

POETRY

'Tis The Seasons – Poems to Lift Your Holiday Spirits

the flower shop on the corner – A Spring Poetry Anthology

the ocean waves – A Summer Poetry Anthology

the leaves fall – An Autumnal Poetry Anthology

Proud to Be – A Pride Poetry Collection

Words for the Earth – A Poetry Project

Dear You – Poems Through the Heart

THE STAND OUT SERIES

Stand Out – The Best of The Red Penguin Collection, Vol. 1

Stand Out – The Best of The Red Penguin Collection, Vol. 2

www.ingramcontent.com/pod-product-compliance
Lightning Source LLC
Chambersburg PA
CBHW060555100726
47907CB00005B/1363